# hideaway at the lagoon
# the collection

elsie james

# copyright



Elsiejamesauthor.com

# introduction

***Welcome to a world where the women are curvy and the men are salivating! Lumberjacks, Ranchers, and Mountain Men are waiting to sweep you off your feet.***

***Join Elsie's Newsletter and get a FREE EBook***

Save big with ebook bundles

***Lumberjack Collections***

Lumberjack Lagoon
Return to Lumberjack Lagoon
Hideaway at the Lagoon
Lumberjack Lodge
The Buckner Brothers

***Rancher Collections***

Findlay Farms
Kingridge Ranch

Midnight Kisses at the Ranch

Tiding Family Holidays

***Mountain Men Collections***

The Brewer Brothers

Hotel at Brew by Brewer

Holidays at Brewer

# grumpy lumberjack

*Hideaway at the Lagoon Book One*

# 1
# prologue: ariella astor

So many firsts in such a short time have my stomach in knots as the old man's truck lurches and jumps up the forest road. I'd never even heard of Lumberjack Lagoon before a few weeks ago and now I'm here.

I never thought I'd be desperate enough to accept a ride from a random old man, especially not one named Hank Hemlock. The dude screams small-town serial killer. I never thought I'd live in a tiny town thousands of miles from everything I've ever known. And I most definitely never thought I'd be purchasing a home with a cashier's check... A home. *My* home. If you can even call the A-frame shell of an abandoned cottage a home.

Old Man Hemlock scowls behind the wheel. His face is wrinkled and worn down by time. His eyes have permanent squint lines that make me think he's spent years working outside. I can't imagine botox is big out here, but still. The corners of his mouth are pulled down into a permanent frown. Overall, it's not a great look. But I'm not exactly in a position to judge, especially not today.

There's no doubt that Mr. Hemlock is giving off some uncomfortable vibes. But he was kind enough to pick me up from the train station and drive me all the way out here without killing me or doing any of the other creepy things you see on the news. Of course, he isn't much of a talker and that doesn't help his case. In fact, the man hasn't uttered a single word since we started driving.

In the silence, I think about my sisters and my heart gets heavy. I wonder if they've discovered that I'm gone. I imagine Nadia will be the first to realize it. She's always been the most responsible, next to me, of course. She'll do her due diligence, call around, and contact my former employer. But she won't find any clues until she checks her bookshelf.

*I hope she checks the bookshelf.*

When she's sure she's correct, Nadia will call the twins. There's no telling how Eloise and Roslyn will react. I'm sure it will be hard, but they'll move on eventually. Once enough time has passed and it's safe, I'll reach out to them. This isn't forever, but it's my only option for now.

I look out of the window at the winding path of indistinguishable trees that stretch out in front of us. My road trip buddy is still officially busy grunting at the potholes and my mind wanders again. This time, I think about... *him.* Not the old man, but the scary, dangerous *him* who caused this nightmare in the first place, Doss Blakely and the Red Dirt Brothers Motorcycle Club.

*What's Doss going to do when he realizes I don't belong to him anymore? For starters, he'll try to find me. I learned that the hard way the last time I tried to leave him. But this time is different. He won't be able to, not way out here. Not with the way I vanished and left no trace behind. Even when he or his Red Dirt Brothers question my sisters, they won't have anything to tell him. If I lay low for long enough, he'll move on and I will be finally free.*

A massive bump in the road sends my body flying off the seat.

When I land, the interior of the truck gives off a new round of must. It's a sickening smell made of a combination of sweat and old leather. I crack my window and gulp in the fresh mountain air.

The ridiculousness of my situation pulls a humorless chuckle out of me. I've really done it this time. If the girls from Lady Katherine's Academy could only see me now. They'd never believe that Ariella Astor is in the front seat of an old rusted-out truck with a silent but somehow aggressive lumberjack behind the wheel running from a motorcycle gang. I can hardly believe it myself.

But ten minutes and three turns later, there's no time left to think. The truck comes to an aggressive stop and there's nothing left but the reality of my new life.

The old man holds his hand out. At first, I go in for a hand shake. But that causes his furry eyebrows to pull together in a deep frown. Then I realize it's the cashier's check he's after and I hand it over. My life savings is gone. Just like that.

I try for a smile, but the old man Hemlock's scowl doesn't budge. "Thanks again for picking me up. I'm sure you didn't expect an hours-long ride from the train station to be a part of the deal in selling your cottage."

He lets out an unsettling cackle. "I didn't do it for you. Just wanted to get rid of the cottage. It's a real piece of work. It's cost me a ton over the years, a true money pit. I'll be glad to see it go." His voice is gruff and it sends tingles down my spine.

I clear my throat. "Wonderful, what a… glowing review of the place I just sunk every penny I have into purchasing." I trail off, blowing out a deep breath and drumming my fingers on the door handle.

So maybe it won't be a hidden gem of a home. But that's okay because, in truth, I was never *looking* for a home. I was looking for a place to hide. From the way I've already lost myself in the winding trees around us, I think this place will fit the bill perfectly.

I climb out of the truck and Mr. Hemlock hands me a single key. He unloads what little I brought onto the end of the gravel driveway in a matter of minutes. From there, he's all too eager to get back into his truck.

As I drag my belongings up the path toward the cottage, all I can see is an overgrown mound of ivy under a large tree and an intricate, thatched roof with missing shingles sticking out of the top. The sound of his old truck tires crunching on the gravel disappears in the distance and I swallow hard.

I'm left standing alone in front of the dilapidated cottage. If it weren't for the thin deed of sale in my hands, I'd think I made this whole thing up. But it's real. For better or worse, this place is all mine now.

For a minute, my feet lock themselves to the ground beneath me and my throat runs dry. I'm afraid to admit even to myself that this might have been a mistake. Not that I had many options either way.

I take a few steps forward, approaching the cabin with caution the way you would a wild animal. *Also, please, please, please don't be any wild animals out here.*

When I put a hand on the front porch railing. Its old, splintered, wooden exterior somehow invites me in. The door lets out a strained creak as I push it open. *It isn't exactly a five-star resort, but it has a certain charm to it.*

I step in and the air is cool but stuffy. I get the feeling I'm the first person to see the inside of this place in a very long time. It's an uncomfortable thought for a girl whose idea of roughing it is booking a cheap hotel room. But if this is the cost of freedom, I'm here for it.

I exhale a deep breath that unknots my chest for the first time in weeks. The main room is surprisingly spacious. There's a cozy-ness about it or at least, I imagine there could be over time. The vaulted ceiling and exposed wood beams bring in warmth and make it feel bigger.

The walls are made of rough, knotted pine and immediately I want to Google how to whitewash orange-colored wood. But that's impossible because I couldn't disappear with my cell phone, especially not with the way Doss used it to track my every movement.

I pat the wad of cash in my pocket. The Red Dirt MC's parting gift to me will be enough to help me get settled into a new life there. At least it would've been their parting gift if they knew I swiped it from the safe. They aren't the only ones unafraid to blur the lines of right and wrong.

Tomorrow I'll use the money to get a new phone, a few groceries, and some kind of transportation. I'd like a car, but with the amount of work that needs to be done to make this cottage liveable, I may be more on a bike budget. Either way, I'll be as good as new.

To my right, a small, sage green kitchenette is tucked away in the corner of the room. When I run my hand across the wooden countertops, they're are dull and rough. I turn on the antique faucet and it takes a minute before the icy water sputters out. But it isn't rusted, and that counts for something.

There's a large wood-burning stove at the far end of the room and I go sit beside it. A pile of logs by my feet are ready to be lit and I wonder how long they've been waiting. I wonder how long I'll be here waiting. I wonder what I'm waiting for.

I didn't have the chance to think much beyond getting away from Doss and his threats. Now that I'm free and my sisters are safe in my absence, my future is somewhat of a mystery.

The dusty windows that face the back of the cabin stretch from floor to ceiling and bathe the cottage in natural light. In my other life, a life of boarding school and champagne problems, I would've been creeped out by such an open view. But inexplicably, here in the middle of a forest, all alone, I find peace.

The stunning view of the dense green forest outside truly takes my breath away. The trees tower above as far as the eye can see. Their leaves rustle in the gentle breeze, sunlight dancing on the branches and casting a dappled shade on the forest floor.

Then my eyes settle on the massive, abandoned greenhouse standing watch in the middle of the picturesque windows. It's nearly the size of the cabin itself, it may be even larger. I have to catch my breath. *Is it really mine too?*

I scramble to my feet, grabbing the deed paperwork and flipping through it. Sure enough, my new property line extends well past the glass structure. The greenhouse is mine.

My breath catches in my throat. I can hardly wait to explore it. I feel something like hope prickle in my stomach for the first time in a long time and I spend the rest of the evening dreaming of the new life I'll live in this place.

I watch the sunset and when the darkness of night falls in the forest, I watch that too. With so many windows, it's like I'm sleeping under the stars only without all the bugs and creepy-crawling things.

But when I lay down for my first night in my barely liveable cottage, sleep never comes. Instead, I find myself searching through my boxes for my books the way I have so many times before. Even with my limited space and quick escape, I knew my books had to come. I couldn't bring the whole TBR shelf of course, but a few old favorites made the cut. I've left my home, my sisters, and my past because of him, but I draw the line at my books.

By sunrise, my eyelids are heavy. I lay down on my blanket scooped into a pile in the center of the creaky hardwood floors clutching my books to my chest. My eyes drift to the ceiling. I can imagine the rain pattering against it. I can imagine myself, in a new bed, in a new life tucked into the base of the trees. My thoughts swirl and twist until they settle into one echoing question played over and over on repeat.

*I know I'll be alone, it's the price I had to pay. But will I be lonely?*

My eyes start to get heavy and I drift off. But it's only an hour before a distinct sound from outside has me sitting bolt upright.

"Is that a chainsaw?"

# 2
# ariella

The soggy wet leaves squish through my fingertips and I toss them onto the ground in handfuls. *I'm such a badass these days.* I crank up Beyonce in my headphones and sing along aloud.

"Yes, Bey, girls do run the world." I cheer myself on.

Things are starting to come together. It's been two weeks and I'm officially turning over a new leaf, branching out on my own, and all the other lumberjack-forest puns I can think of out here in Lumberjack Lagoon. I've even gotten used to the distant hum of the lumberjacks using chainsaws in the background.

Today, in another episode of things-the-old-me-would-never-do, I'm up on my roof. I've got two goals, clear my gutters of the accumulated pine needles and don't fall off. The sharp pitch makes both goals fairly unattainable. But I'm hoping for at least one of the two.

It isn't perfect, but this cottage is a far cry from what I walked into the first day. Even though it's quiet, it's starting to feel a lot more like home. For starters, there's a turquoise beach cruiser that officially belongs to me parked on the porch. With its narrow smooth tires, it's not as ideal as say, a mountain bike or a car. But for now, it gets me into the heart of Lumberjack Lagoon and back.

Besides, riding a bike everywhere is forcing me to literally stop and smell the roses. I'm not exactly athletic and I've found a few stops on my path that I like to use to force the fresh forest air into my lungs. The sense of calm is oddly exhilarating. I'm not ready to do anything crazy like take up hiking. But I guess I expected to be out of sorts and on edge out here in the great wide-open space and that isn't the case.

The trees tower above me and there's an odd comfort in hiding under their canopy of shade. I can hear leaves rustling in the gentle breeze. I can breathe. After what I've been through, I don't take that for granted.

I crawl to the next mushy pile, in a move that's straight out of the Broadway show *Cats.* But the stupid, sopping, mess of leaves are still just out of reach. "Come on, cooooomeeee on." I'm in a full extension and worried my black yoga pants are about to give up on me when I get the distinct feeling of eyes on me.

Initially, I shake it off because... that's crazy. I know there isn't anyone out here. I'm sure it's some sort of PTSD that I've gotten compliments from the Red Dirt MC. No one is out here because I don't think anyone could find this place if they tried.

"You're gonna kill yourself like that." A man's burly voice reverberates in my ears, by passing Beyonce and shaking me to my core.

For a moment, my heart stops. Then I move with a start, panicking and bolting upright. My foot, desperate to find balance, smashes into a wooden shingle. The shingle doesn't stand a chance. It snaps like a twig and before I know it, I'm cascading right off of the roof.

I let out an awkward yelp then scratch and claw at the shingles on my way down. *Because using them for support worked so well last time.* Unsurprisingly, they don't slow me down at all, but I manage to pull a few of them off with me.

*I never got to transform the greenhouse* is all I can think as I plummet towards the ground.

My heart races and I close my eyes, bracing for the impact. But the ground never comes. Instead, I find myself floating in a pair of strong arms. When I open my eyes, I see that I'm just inches away from the squared jawline of an extremely handsome lumberjack.

His muscles bulge out of his flannel shirt. He smiles, and I feel a warmth spread through my chest. His teeth are so white I think I could see my own reflection in them if my head wasn't spinning. My eyes come back into focus and I'm stunned by his perfection. For a moment, I can't speak at all.

I freeze in place all over again. His eyes are dark and brooding, but not intimidating in the way they should be for a man this large. When he puts me down gently on the ground, I look up at him.

It's no wonder he caught me, the man's not that much shorter than the bottom of the roofline. *Don't say that out loud Ariella, be cool.*

I take a deep breath, trying to steady my nerves. I open my mouth to speak, but my heart is still racing, jumbling my thoughts. I feel a little lightheaded and I don't know if it's the fall or his smile that's messing with me.

The lumberjack clears his throat and gestures to my foot. "There's a pretty good scrape and it's already swollen. You might need to go in. Let me take a look at your ankle." He squats down, taking my foot in his massive hands. "If so, I can take you."

I ignore the blood dripping onto my sock. "Go in, like to the hospital? No, really, that's totally fine and if I do need to go, I can just take my bike."

He tilts his head and shoots me a look with one arched eyebrow that tells me he thinks I might be crazy. "You'll ride your bike with an ankle the size of a softball to the hospital?" He pauses then lets out a chuckle. "That's the stupidest thing I've ever heard. Almost as bad as doing yoga on a roof. Where's your car?" His laugh is guttural as he teases me and it's sexy as hell.

"Oh, I did have a car. But when I went to leave on the morning of my big move, it wasn't working. So I figured it out without one. Now I'm here." I swallow back my discomfort at the topic. "And just so you know, it wasn't yoga. I was cleaning my gutters."

"Right." He raises an eyebrow at me.

I brush a strand of hair behind my ear. "But thank you for catching me. It's nice to meet you, I'm—"

He cuts me off, biting back a smile. "I'm Caleb Greenwood and your Ariella Astor. You bought this place with a cash transaction. You're from out of town, but you traveled without your car. So what I don't know is what you're really doing here."

My jaw drops open. "How did you know?"

He touches the outside of my ankle and I wince. A sharp pain shoots up my leg and his brows furrow in concern.

"Sweetheart, the first rule of living in Lumberjack Lagoon is that there aren't any secrets here. I don't know who you are or what you're running from, but best keep it to yourself if you don't want it getting out." He gets to his feet. "It isn't broken, but I think it might be sprained. Let me carry you inside."

Before I can protest, Caleb scoops me back up into his arms. He carries me effortlessly towards the cottage. I should be totally terrified, I know that. I'm out in the woods where I don't know anyone and now even my ankle has given up on me. But surprisingly, I can't muster up a single ounce of anxiety. Instead, I revel in the warmth and safety in his arms.

He sets me down on my countertop, propping my ankle up on a stack of books. His eyes fill with concern. Then he pulls his shirt off over his head. My jaw drops at the sight of his chiseled chest and I can't look away. He runs the faucet, soaking his shirt in cold water and then wraps it around the cut on my ankle. I try to make small talk, but it's no use with those muscles staring me in the face. He looks like a sexy Paul Bunyon and right now, I look like my own scum twin.

Caleb walks to the light switch and flips it on. When nothing happens, he mumbles something about an electrical panel and walks into the garage. I do my part by gawking at him and staying shell shocked into silence. When he returns, Caleb's got a sour look on his face. By sour I mean, brooding, pensive, and still sexy as hell.

"You need light bulbs… and weather stripping. I wouldn't be surprised if you don't get a leak from the shingle issue." He isn't making eye contact and I can't tell if Caleb is talking to me or to himself.

"Well, I'm planning on watching a whole lot of YouTube videos to figure a few things out. But I can change the lightbulbs. I just need to get a ladder next time I'm out and I'll be all set." I nod with what I think is a reassuring look."

"You don't have a ladder in a place like this?" He tilts his head toward the peak of the ceiling.

"You're pretty judgy for a guy that doesn't have a shirt. Don't you think?" I bite back a giggle.

He smiles and a deep set dimple appears on his cheek. "How'd you get on the roof without a ladder?"

"I used a stump I found out back and shimmied up the drain-pipe from there."

His forehead pinches together. "Okay, we need to talk about a few things. First off, no more creative climbing for DIY projects. Let's get your ankle feeling better and then I'll help you with whatever you need. I'm a lumberjack, climbing is what we do. Secondly, you can't be so trusting."

His first comment makes me laugh, there's something about his mix of grumpy and sweet that's captured my heart. But Caleb's second comment catches me totally off guard. I've been accused of a few things over the years, but never of trusting. I've seen too much for that to be the case.

"You got into a car with Hank Hemlock. I don't ever want you alone with him again and he'll be around. He lives close to you. The dilapidated lodge just up the road is his. He's an asshole for a lot of reasons, not least of which is selling you a cottage in this condition. He's a bad guy." The sincerity in his eyes makes goosebumps crawl across my arms.

I thought something was off about the old man. Maybe I can trust my instincts again."So you're the good guy in this story."

"Wrong again sweetheart, You'd be smart to stay away from me too. In fact, I'd better get going." Caleb takes a step away from the counter. "Rest, ice, compression, and elevation for the rest of the day."

But that can't possibly be true. This man is all good, but is he too good to be true?

Falling for a random lumberjack is the absolute last thing I need in my life right now. Still, as he turns to leave, I can't help but watch him go, and not just because he's got jeans that cling to his backside so tightly it leaves nothing to the imagination. There's something kind behind his gruff exterior and I'm desperate to know more about him.

I thank him again and he gives me a subtle nod. Then Caleb Greenwood is on his way out of my world just as quickly as he entered it. When he reaches the hollow front door that I painted a pink-blush color, the handle rotates in his hand.

"It doesn't lock, I just stack books in front of it for now," I call out.

Caleb turns back toward me. "Have a good night. My brother Kai and I will be by in the morning."

I blink in surprise. "For what?

"Can't have you living in a place like this."

He walks out of the front door without any explanation and his words swirl in my mind all night. *He isn't serious. He can't be. Can he? No. The last thing I need is to be the girl who fell off her roof and also reads too much into a comment.*

By the time night falls, I drag my books in front of the door and try to forget all about Caleb. But I fall asleep with butterflies still knocking in my stomach nonetheless.

The next morning, I get up extra early and put on mascara for the first time since arriving in Lumberjack Lagoon just in case. On the off chance, Caleb actually shows up this morning, I don't want to look like a total hot mess. Though logically, I can't imagine he will.

It's still chilly outside despite the morning sun and I'm sitting in my kitchen sipping the hottest of teas when I hear the rumble of a truck pulling down my gravel driveway.

# 3
# caleb

"Why are we here again?" My brother Kai heaves the heavy toolbox out of the back of my truck bed.

"We're helping someone who's new to town to fix up old man Hemlock's shit hole of a cottage. What's so hard to grasp about that?" My words come out in a bark.

"It isn't hard to imagine *me* doing something like this. But *you*? Finding a damsel in distress isn't your style." Kai laughs but I don't join in.

"Would you shut up and let Buck out of the truck?" I shake my head, but I know Kai isn't wrong.

There's something about Ariella's mix of innocence and strength that left me absolutely captivated yesterday. She makes me want to show up for her in a way I'm not used to showing up for anyone. I don't really care for the feeling, but here I am.

I head for the front door with Buck rushing out ahead of me, tail wagging, and Kai hot on my heels. By the time I reach the hollow shell of a front door, Ariella's already got it open. She looks stunning in a pair of jeans and a flowy top that I sure as hell won't be able to get out of my head.

"Good morning." Her smile stretches from ear to ear and I'm happy to see she seems to be moving around on her ankle just fine. "I can't believe you came. I've got a fresh batch of scones for you and hot water on the stove. Do you like your tea loose leaf or bagged?"

I pause, scowling at her odd question. "I don't think I've ever made a cup of tea in my entire thirty-four years... I—"

"Loose leaf for me." Kai cuts me off then hits Ariella with a too-big smile that makes me want to punch him in the face as he steps around me. "I'm Kai Greenwood, it's nice to meet you."

I let out an exaggerated sigh. He's like this every single time we meet a new woman, let alone one as hot as Ariella. "This is my brother Kai, a lifelong tea enthusiast, apparently." Sarcasm drips from my sentence.

Her eyebrows arch up as she takes him in. "Another Greenwood brother, what a nice surprise."

I hate the way Kai manages to pull a smile from her lips.

He continues, "There's another of us too, Cain, but he's deployed. So you're stuck with the two of us today." Kai clinks his mug with Ariella's without even bothering to hide his self-satisfied smile.

"I'd love to offer you a seat, but that box of books is probably the best I can do at the moment," she says.

"Works for me." Kai looks like an overgrown toddler when he plops down onto the box. "We've got some slabs over at Timber Logging that'd make some pretty good furniture..."

My eyes flick back and forth between them at their chatty little conversation. *Where the hell does my brother get off thinking that it's okay to just swoop in and flirt with the woman I brought him here to help?*

Ariella being the absolute angel she is offers us what has got to be the most delicious scone I've ever had in my whole damn life. She refills two cups of tea, one for herself, and the other for my dumbass brother. She makes a stack of books in the center of the kitchen and drapes it with a towel. Then she puts the teapot on top of it. I've got to get this girl a proper table.

Buck sits back, watching all this too. When he gets tired of waiting his turn to get attention from Ariella, he lunges forward. He puts his massive paws on the stack of books and topples them over. He's an overgrown puppy of a Bernese Mountain Dog and I love him, but he isn't exactly graceful.

"Hey, you sit," I growl and Buck gives in, immediately lowering himself to the ground.

She leans down and runs her hands through his fur. I try unsuccessfully to pull my eyes away from the mouth watering cleavage peeking out of the top of her shirt.

Ariella giggles and squeals with delight. "Oh, I love this guy. He's such a sweetheart. How long have you had him?"

Her question hits like a punch to the gut. For a moment, even Kai is stunned into silence. My brother and I shoot looks at each other in the silence as a swell of dread builds in my stomach.

"A while," I say.

Ariella seems to get it and she backs off the topic. But Kai can't leave well enough alone.

He clears his throat. "Buck used to belong to our other brother, Kameron. But when Kameron passed, Buck became all of ours. He was just a pup at the time. So he comes to work at the Timber yard with us now during the day and rotates through our houses. When Cain gets back from deployment, he'll take him for a while. Right now, Buck's stuck with me and Caleb. But it's obvious he likes me the most." He winks in Ariella's direction.

We haven't even gotten our tools out yet and I'm already ready for Caleb to leave. This guy is unreal. "Kai enough—" I start, shaking my head.

But now it's Ariella's turn to cut me off. "I'm sorry to hear that. You know, I actually lost a younger brother a few years back too. It's tough. It still seems like yesterday." She nods thoughtfully and I don't miss the swell of compassion that flickers in her eyes.

"So you're alone now and that's why you moved?" Kai finishes his second cup of tea with a grin, like dead leaves in water is the best thing he's ever tasted.

Ariella blushes and tucks a strand of hair behind her ear and it makes me roll my eyes.

"Not exactly, I have three sisters too, but they…" She trails off, shaking her head.

I cut my eyes at Kai. "Sorry, this guy has no manners, not an ounce of tact. It's hard to believe we grew up in the same house. He should stick to being a lumberjack because investigative reporting isn't it for him. Let's get to work. This place isn't going to fix itself. Ariella I've got a list here based on what I saw yesterday, but if there's anything you want to add, let me know and we'll get you squared away."

She stands too. "Thank you. The biggest help would be the door and window locks. I'd like to be able to sleep a little better at night and I think that would do the trick. Everything else I can figure out at some point, I'm sure of it."

"I like your confidence, but there ain't no way you're getting back up on that roof. As for the locks, consider it done." As the words leave my lips, I can't help but wonder what she's hiding or maybe who she's hiding from.

The thought of someone making this woman uncomfortable sends a fire coursing through me. I'm enamored with her and completely overwhelmed by a visceral need to protect her.

For the next few hours, we get to work on the cottage. Kai patches up holes in the roof while I take a look at the water pressure. I move from one window to the next, securing them as best I can on the rickety old frames.

Every chance I get, I steal glances at Ariella. She's got a timeless quality to her beauty. It's honest and effortless. She laughs easily and works hard. Ariella has an intoxicating mix of humility and strength. I've never been so taken with someone I hardly know, but I can't deny the pull I feel towards her. Being around her for one day could never be enough.

When I move to her bedroom, the door is blocked by a massive moving box and I let out a chuckle. "More books? You've got to be kidding me. I'm adding a bookshelf to the list. We can put one one in the living room, no problem. We could go wall to wall on either side of the fireplace. How big do you want it?"

Her face lights up. "You're kidding! I'd love an entire bookshop, but you don't have to do that."

As soon as she says the words, I consider it done. My mind goes to work on all the ways I can turn Ariella's dream of a bookshop into a reality. She deserves it.

I flip on the lightswitch near the doorway. "I've got to ground all the electricity in the whole cottage. Otherwise, you're going to blow the place up. I can't believe Hemlock left you with all this, it's a damn hazzard. I'll add that to the list too. We won't get through it all today, but we've got a lot of family here in Lumberjack Lagoon. I'll round some up to help us get this done."

She takes a step toward me and I like having her this close. "Thank you Caleb, I don't know why you're helping me but I hope you know I appreciate it." Ariella runs a hand across my forearm and it sends whips of fire crackling through me.

"You're welcome."

The door pushes open and Kai and the dog burst in through the back door. Ariella steps away from me and Buck barrels toward us. Both of them stick their noses right back into my business and my moment with Ariella is officially over. I suppose it's probably for the best. I don't have a great track record when it comes to keeping people safe.

"We're going to be able to get a tractor down here, trench our the downspouts. I just made a few calls." Kai starts, then turns to Ariella. "Anyone with the last name Oakes is related to us and this town is crawling with them. Our cousins have got an ongoing initiative to rebuild Lumberjack Lagoon. Lumberjills Coffee Shop, the market, and the Flannel and Frills bed and breakfast all exist thanks to them, so they are more than willing to help."

"Thank you Kai, that's really sweet. I'm not used to asking for help like this, but I'm so happy you're here." She smiles, but it stops at her cheeks.

Buck bounds across the living room. But trying to stop himself from sliding on the old hardwoods proves to be impossible. He puts his paws forward, coming to a sliding stop and sending a tower of books cascading into the air.

Ariella rushes toward them, picking up books between laughs, and I do too. When my hand brushes hers heat floods through me again. This time, I'm overwhelmed with the need to kiss her, but I hold back and keep myself together.

Something in me tells me that she's breakable and I'm a bull in a china shop. Proceeding with caution is the way to this woman's heart even if I shouldn't be the one heading for it. I don't know what she's been through, but she needs time. That much is obvious and that isn't a problem for me. I'd give her anything.

And so we settle into it. I spend the next two weeks racing home from my shifts at Timber Logging only to change and head straight to Ariella's cottage. Sometimes I bring Kai or one of my already-married cousins when I need the help. But most days, I go alone.

There are times we laugh and talk about everything under the sun. We work on her cottage and learn everything about each other. Ariella bakes me all sorts of pastries and has me drinking tea. On other days we don't say anything at all. But somewhere in those quiet moments, Ariella becomes my favorite person.

# 4
# ariella

"Okay, so the chainsaw is going to lead you with its teeth unless you lead it first." Caleb has gone full lumberjack on me today and I love it. He turns back to look at me. "Sweetheart, you've got to put the goggles on! Dammit, you're determined to hurt yourself."

I bite back a giggle. "I have sunglasses, it's the same."

"No—" Caleb takes another step toward me.

But I cut him off by pulling the ripcord. The chainsaw fires up and it stops him in his tracks. Caleb yells something that I can't make out over the sound of the engine, but I don't stop. I sink the edge of the blade into the side of the tree stump and zip the top off. It's exhilarating.

"I can see why you like your job so much," I yell. "This is a good time!"

When I turn back to him, Caleb makes his eyes big in an exaggerated gesture that makes me laugh.

"Why was that so hot?" He lets out a chuckle.

I let out a giggle and shake my head. "That's so much fun. I feel like I'm ready to carve this stump into a bear or a bunny or something cooler."

He takes the chainsaw out of my hands. "Come on, put that down before someone loses a limb, you timber beast. I'm taking you on a walk through these woods. If you're gonna turn your greenhouse into a bookshop someday, you should at least know what's out here around it."

"Okay, let's do it." I step toward him, my feet crunching into the soft forest floor. "But just so you know, I've watched about a thousand YouTube videos about this land and I've read a few books about Lagoons so I may be able to teach you a thing or two. Just don't want you to be surprised by all my outdoor knowledge." I shrug.

He furrows his eyebrows at me and shakes his head. "Get over here."

I'm drawn to Caleb like a magnet. The truth is, I'd go anywhere with him. We walk side by side through the majestic woods, a canopy of green hanging over our heads. I keep pace with him as he expertly navigates the trees and we take turns pointing out all things flowering in the forest.

Getting to know Caleb has been a whirlwind of bliss. He's confident and smoldering. He can be grumpy, but the man has a heart like a teddy bear. The days have flown by with him in them.

When we round a bend into an open meadow, he looks at me. His eyes move up and down across me, appraising, and I think, liking what he sees. His laser sharp attention trained on me makes me blush.

Caleb starts, "You didn't grow up here. You have a family that presumably means a lot to you, but you don't see them. You don't have a job, but you bought your house cash with no plan. You're breathtaking, but your single. Nothing about you makes any sense. You're a woman of mystery."

"I guess I am when you put it like that," I bite back my smile. Keeping things from him has gotten increasingly difficult.

"Tell me something about you. It doesn't have to be all of it, but you've met everyone in my world at this point. I'm so curious about you. You're my favorite person and you've got to give me something." There's a kindness in his tone that tugs at my heart.

All I want is to tell him everything, but I have to be careful. I look away from his intense stare searching for the right words. "Well, my sisters and I went to a boarding school in a tiny farm town. I suppose that's something interesting. After my parents passed, my aunt sent the four of us girls off. It couldn't have been easy to take on five kids, so I don't hold it against her. But it was an odd way to grow up. I think that's why I've never wanted kids. I feel like I already raised my sisters. The school was girls only, so my brother stayed back. He lived with my aunt and uncle on the ranch. He worked as a farmhand and ended up getting himself mixed up in all sorts of bad things..." I trail off, stopping myself.

It's too easy to share with Caleb. He pulls it out of me. If I don't watch myself, I'll be telling him everything before I have a chance to think it through. He told me himself that secrets fly through Lumberjack Lagoon and I don't want to test the theory.

"Boarding school, wow. I didn't see that coming. But now that you mention it, I think I can see the boarding school girl in you. Were there uniforms, there were uniforms, weren't there? Damn I bet that was hot." He lets out an easy laugh, ducks under a branch, and holds it back for me to follow. "I know you said your brother passed, but tell me more about these sisters of yours."

"No way, it's your turn." I cross my arms and smirk up at him. "Tell me about your favorite spot in the woods. You grew up out here, so you must have one place that stands out above the others in your mind."

He tugs at his beard and his eyes go dark. "Hmm, good question. Well I wouldn't call it a favorite, but I can show you where I go to think."

"I'd like that."

There's a somberness to his tone that I don't expect and we walk a winding path in silence. I wonder about this lumberjack who has come out of nowhere and stolen my heart. There's a hurt in his eyes that I can't put my finger on, but it's undoubtedly there. What's breaking his heart, or who?

When we approach a majestic old oak beside the bend in a road that I had no idea was back here, he stops. Caleb places his massive palm on the bark and takes a sharp inhale of breath. When he does, the forest seems to quiet around us.

Then Caleb sits on the stump of a cut-down tree beside the large oak. I follow suit, sitting on a boulder. It's peaceful out here and it isn't hard to see why he likes it. I take in the serenity around me. I notice the ferns that spring up in unexpected places and the dense green as far as the eye can see. When Caleb finally turns to me his eyes are dark and brooding. The air grows heavy and I hold my breath.

He clears his throat. "I told you from the start that I'm not a good guy. This is where I prove it. You should know before I go falling for you like this, it isn't right... This tree is where my brother Kameron died and the truth is, it's my fault."

His raw admission takes my breath away. I watch in stunned silence as every emotion flickers across his face. I see a glimpse of loss followed by sadness and finally anger. He's an untapped well of hurt and I can't look away. My eyes lock on his. I lean in toward him, approaching the subject with caution.

"What happened?" For someone who came here hiding everything, it's a bold question. But I can't help myself. I want to know everything about Caleb, the good parts and the parts he hides away.

"I was in a fight down at a bar in town over something stupid and I called him up. I told him I needed him. I knew he'd drop everything and come even though he was getting ready for deployment the next morning. It was a selfish call to begin with. But what I didn't know was that he'd been drinking. I should have, hell I would have if I'd taken even half a second to think it through. He was just like our dad, always one beer too many in. But Kameron didn't hesitate. He hopped in his truck to fight alongside me. He didn't make it to the bar that night. He didn't make it past this damn round in the bend. This tree stopped him. This tree stopped everything." Caleb takes another sharp inhale of breath and shakes his head.

Without giving it a single thought, I reach across and take his hand in mine. Losing a brother is a pain I know all too well and the Caleb's shattered omission breaks my heart. When I finally speak, my words come out in a whisper. "Your brother sounds a lot like you."

"I'd have traded places with him in a second. He was a much better man than I am. He was a lumberjack, a soldier, and one hell of a cook when he got behind the grill. He would've never put me in the same situation. He didn't hurt people the way I do." Caleb turns away from me and the pain in his tone is palpable. "It's a damn shame."

We stay there in silence for a long time while the sounds of the forest slowly filter back in. There's nothing I can say to make Caleb feel better. I know that from experience. So I hold space for him. I let him be sad and I sit with him in the weight of his emotions.

I stand and walk toward the stump Caleb is sitting on. Without a single word, I wrap my arms around him. At first, his body goes rigid, but I don't lose my resolve. I stay there holding him together so he can fall apart.

Eventually, he does. The floodgates open and I feel his body relax into mine. Caleb buries his face into me and holds on so tight I swear I can feel his heartbeat in my own chest.

This beautiful man is showing me a depth of character I didn't expect to find. I feel connected to him beyond what is rational. Being with him in such an intimate setting feels right. The word love whips irrationally through my mind, but I don't dare utter it aloud. Not when my life is such a mess.

But holding it in doesn't stop my heart from breaking for the loss in Caleb's life, and for mine too. Through it, I don't let go. Time stands still while I hold him in a beautiful, painful embrace that means so much more than any words can say.

When he finally lets go, I put my hands on either side of his face and tilt his chin up toward mine. When our eyes meet, I speak clearly. I want him to know that I mean every word. "I'm not afraid Caleb, you are a good man and I know you will never hurt me."

And I do know.

Somehow amid all the bad choices I've made in the past with men, I'm overwhelmed with confidence in the man in front of me. For a moment, I let myself get carried away. Without another thought, I press my lips against his. The electricity that constantly hums in the air between us ignites and the kiss leaves me breathless.

I feel the spark whip through every inch of my body. Caleb lets out a soft moan, but I can tell he's holding back. Though the growing bulge between his legs tells me he doesn't want to. So when his lips part, I slip my tongue into his mouth, and kiss him with reckless abandon.

That's what it takes to love this man back to life. From there, Caleb's hands plant themselves on my waist and he pulls me onto his lap. When I'm straddling him, I can feel the zing of his erection through denim pressing against me and the wet spot on my underwear grows.

Caleb's fingertips roam my body, digging into my hair and running up and down my back. The sensation is pure heaven. He deepens our kiss into a dance that leaves me desperate for more.

# 5
# ariella

We spend hours together in the forest kissing and writhing against each other until Caleb pulls back. He doesn't trust himself to love me and that's not a spell my kiss could break.

In a last ditch effort, I asked him if love was a requirement. But the idea of casually sleeping together in the woods wasn't something he could entertain. He told me that I'm so much more than one night to him.

His rejection was the gentlemanly thing to do. But who wants a gentleman when it's been months since I've had sex. Caleb's got me so wound up that all I can think about is feeling him inside of me.

In the end I have no choice other than to settle for walking hand in hand back toward my cottage. By the time my cottage comes back into sight, the sun is going down. Everything is washed in a brilliant, golden, glow. Walking beside Caleb feels like a dream.

But when we round the bend, something catches me off guard. I look out into the distance, trying to make out the shape in the fiery sunlight. When it becomes clear, I'm startled by what I see.

The truck is big and white. The windows are tinted a midnight black and the tires are way too big to be from around here. That's got to be a farm truck. If I didn't know any better, I'd say it looks an awful lot like the one Doss used to drive. My blood runs cold. "There's a truck parked at the bottom of the hill. I wonder who's truck that is."

"What truck?" Caleb turns his head as if he's hardly noticed.

I try to hide the urgency in my voice. "That white truck parked just up the road. It looks... I've just never seen it over here is all. You know, I'm ready to be inside for the night."

Caleb inhales, shaking his head. His muscles somehow seem to swell even bigger on the spot. He pulls me toward him, swapping sides and putting himself between me and the truck in the distance. "Go ahead inside, I'm gonna have a quick chat with whoever is in that truck."

"Caleb, don't it might be... a dangerous situation." My heart rate ticks up. Guilt swirls in me. If I'm going to let Caleb in, it needs to be all the way. He could be walking into a situation he isn't at all prepared to face.

"I'm dangerous too." He winks at me and disappears through the front door.

I head for the porch too, but then I stop myself. If it is Doss, seeing me with another man will only make the situation worse. Just like that, the cloud of hormonal bliss that has been lingering around me evaporates.

This is real... too real. I can't let myself slip up like this. I hold my breath until the front door opens again. Caleb returns with a big smile safe and unharmed. I let out a sigh of relief.

He shrugs. "The truck is nothing. Someone is going to look at the lodge. It seems like this cottage isn't the only place the old man Hemlock is looking to get rid of." He sits on the couch beside me and puts a heavy hand on my thigh. "Are you going to tell me what the hell you're doing way out here and why you're so scared?"

I hesitate for a moment, but it's no use. The truth crashes out of me like a tidal wave. "I used to date someone who would do terrible things to me. He started by following me, calling my work to confirm I was where I said I'd be. I didn't like it, but I dealt with it. Then it escalated from there. He started using trackers to keep tabs on me. He'd play mind games. He's caused me to lose more than one job and scared everyone out of my life. His name is Doss and he's the absolute worst. He's threatened my sisters too over the years. It's like his entire goal was to make sure I couldn't be anything without him. In a way it worked." I shake my head.

"What an absolute asshole." Caleb's fists clench into balls.

I continue, "It doesn't stop there. He's a high-ranking member of a motorcycle club that's found themselves on the wrong side of the law. They've made people disappear and I know they're capable of doing it again. His guys are everywhere around Findlay, in the police station, and all around town. You can't escape them, they can make your life hell and they did."

"Someone needs to stop this guy. He can't just run around thinking he's above the law. I'd like to see someone pull some bull-shit like that in Lumberjack Lagoon. Ha! It just wouldn't happen."

I swallow back the dry words as they crawl out of my throat. "That's what I'm doing here. I'm stepping away before he can burn me again. By disappearing, I've let him adjust his focus. Without me or information about me, he has no reason to stalk my sisters or worse and he can't do it to me either if he can't find me."

Caleb turns to me, taking my hands in his. "Sweetheart, you can't live your life like this. Running and hiding out are only going to take you so far. He can't be everywhere. This dip-shit isn't nearly as powerful as you're giving him credit for. And what about your sisters? Don't you miss them?"

"Every. Single. Day."

# 6
# caleb

Ariella deserves a life free from that asshole, the thought of her hiding out here due to fear makes me sick. Rage courses through me. At that moment I make a decision that I will honor for the rest of my life.

*This woman will be safe and I'm going to make sure of it.* I'm going to help her get her life back. I'm going to find her sisters and reunite them. The plan plays out in my mind as if it's already happened. I'm ready to take action, but the look on Ariella's face tells me that right now all she needs is to be held.

I pull her into my chest and make another snap decision. "I'm staying here tonight." I reach around her, flip on the kettle, and make myself comfortable. "Go take a shower, read a book, do whatever it is you need to do to feel like a normal person. I'm gonna sit right here for as long as it takes. Then, I'll kiss you goodnight and sleep on the couch. It isn't a request, go do what you need to do."

She looks up at me and those doe eyes go misty. "Really? Caleb, thank you. I won't say no to that. I haven't been sleeping much and I hate to admit that, but it's unsettling to think about him."

"Sweetheart, I'm gonna promise you right now, no one's coming in here tonight. To get to you, they'd have to come through me and I'd like to see them try." I wink at her but my promise is as serious as they come.

Ariella gives me a smile of relief that breaks my heart before she disappears into the shower. I wonder how long she's been holding onto that stress. *What kind of a man puts someone as kind as Ariella in that position?* The thought sends another jolt of anger coursing through me. *What kind of name is Doss anyway? The dude had no choice but to be an asshole with a name like that.*

I use the free time to take inventory of her cottage. The brown leather couch Kai brought over is working out just fine and the rocking chair is too. With her blankets and pillows thrown all over it, the living room almost looks like a proper home.

I get out my phone and make a list of all the issues that still need repair. Then I shoot a few texts to Kai and my best friend Garrison. I ask them for their schedules and we get a few work days on the books.

Walking through Ariella's cottage it's amazing how every inch of it screams her name. What's even more astonishing is the way she's filled up my entire life. She's constantly on my mind and in the background of everything I do. Ariella is everything that matters to me.

I'm settled onto the couch when she appears in the doorway with her still-wet hair, boxer shorts, and matching tank top with no bra. My eyes rake unabashedly up and down her body. I like the way my stare pulls a blush from her cheeks. I pick up the too-fuzzy blanket from the couch and hold it open to her.

A slow growing smile stretches across her face. "Give me one more minute, I'm gonna make some tea."

"The kettle's already hot. Go pour yourself some. When you're done, we're gonna watch a movie and then you're going to sleep."

But Ariella doesn't go toward the kitchen. Instead, she takes a step toward me. Her eyelids flutter shut. When she opens them there's a sexy smile playing on her lips. "What if I don't *want* to sleep?"

She saunters toward me all tits and curves under thin fabric that drive me wild and I have to catch my breath. My dick is still half hard from earlier and I don't know how much I can take.

Ariella stands in front of me, heat radiating off of her. My heart races as she peels off one article of clothing after the next. Every inch of her body is more perfect than the last, my desire for her burns through me.

"Please Caleb, I need to be close to you right now." Her voice is a whisper and the sound of my name on those full lips sends me into overdrive.

I blow a deep breath out, my mouth watering at the sight of her. "Come here." I reach my arms out, pulling her toward me. An intense desire to possess her overwhelms me. I'm ready to claim her and from the look on her face, she's more than ready to let me.

She makes the rest of the way toward me dropping articles of clothing. By the time she reaches me, she's fully naked. I can't look away. Ariella straddles me and this time, I can't pull my pants off fast enough.

They hit the floor along with my shirt and from there, it's a frenzy. My hands roam her body, wandering the round of her curves and grazing every inch of exposed skin. Her breath quickens as I kiss her neck and shoulders and my hands roam down her back.

Her body quivers as my fingertips explore her soft lines. Ariella is intoxicating. I use my tongue to make my way across her body, taking my time. When I get to her breasts, I slip them into my mouth one at a time. I suck each nipple until they go hard and erect in my mouth.

I need her as much as she needs me. Ever since I lost my brother, I've been a hollow shell of a man. Being this close to her reminds me that I'm alive. I feel it in every part of me. The way her breath on my neck makes me come unglued. The way my mouth waters as I trace the shape of her curves. The way my dick springs up with the weight of her body on my lap.

Ariella throws her head back, moaning softly in pleasure as I devour her. My hands move down her stomach to her hips. I wander lower and lower until my fingers play across her inner thighs. I use a gentle touch on her delicate skin and run my hand across her already drenched slit.

I tease her with my fingertips and Ariella moans my name into the high ceiling. The sound of my name being chanted into the night drives me wild and my dick burns with the need to be inside of her. I stroke her with my fingers, tracing circles across her swollen nub before plunging inside.

Feeling her slick against me makes my manhood swell and pulsate. I love the way her body responds to my touch. My desire to be inside of her is almost too much to handle. I put a hand on her back and move Ariella onto the couch beside me.

Pushing her legs open, I drop to my knees. I bury my tongue inside of her and the taste of her sweetness on my lips has me desperate for more. I stay there, lapping at her, hungry to see her come unglued.

Ariella's fingertips dig into the back of my scalp and she bucks her hips against my face. I can feel the tension rising in her as her orgasm builds and I don't let up until she's begging for more friction. When she's ready, I crawl up her body and our skin becomes one.

"Are you okay? Is this what you want?" My words are a growl and she nods, her eyes pleading for more.

"Caleb, yes. I need you inside of me."

I don't need to be told twice. Lining myself up, I enter her in a single thrust. Ariella's walls move and stretch around me. We're a perfect fit. I love the way she quivers and tenses with pleasure. She takes all of me and my tip swells with desire.

When Ariella clenches along my length, it drives me wild. I thrust inside again, pounding in and out in perfect rhythm. We stay there for what feels like a lifetime. Being with this woman is unlike anything I've ever experienced. She's captivated me and I can't get enough.

One thing is for sure, there isn't any going back now. Life before Ariella doesn't exist anymore. She's shown me a world I never thought was possible and I'm never going to let her go. Here in this cottage with Ariella, I'm among the living again. I'm overwhelmed by the hope of what a future with her could hold. I'm worthy of the chance I've been given.

Her walls tighten around me and Ariella's body racks with tremors as our pleasure intensifies. I can feel myself getting closer and closer to the edge until all of a sudden, I no longer can hold back.

She wraps her legs around my waist. I lose control of myself, slamming into her as she bucks her hips up to meet mine and screams my name. When Ariella throws her head back and cries out in pleasure I know she's reaching her peak.

Thank god she does, because I let go too. I explode, sinking into her with one last, deep thrust and grunting my release into the night. I punch into her shooting hot streams and claiming her. Ariella tilts her hips up and bears down. She wants all of me, and I give it to her rough and uninhibited until the last drop.

# 7
# ariella

Caleb has me two more times before the sun comes up. Then he takes me out for breakfast at the crack of dawn before he heads to work. But somehow I'm not tired. I've made the classic move of replacing good sleep with incredible sex and it's a nice change of pace.

Only, the way Caleb held me into the early hours of the morning tells me that this thing between us could never be just sex. He's single handedly shown me what love should feel like and that is something I'll never take for granted.

It's still early when Caleb drops me off at my cottage before leaving for his shift at Timber Logging. I'm irrationally sad to see him go, but I get to watch him put on the his gear and that feels like a win. It's wild how effortlessly his charm spills over when he's wearing flannel and climbing gear.

I find that I've become obsessed with his every move. I love the way he knows my body and the way I come to life beneath his touch. Caleb has come into my world like a whirlwind and made every part of it better. I'm insatiable. I can't get enough of him.

I flip on the kettle then float down the hall to my bedroom. My newfound joy makes me wish I could call my sisters and share it with them. I know they'd love Caleb. In fact, they might love everything about Lumberjack Lagoon.

But the bittersweet truth is I can't have both the new love in my life and the familiar love of my sisters if I want everyone to stay safe. Caleb is incredible, but he's only one man and a good one at that. The men in the Red Dirt Brothers MC don't play by the same rules as the rest of society. There's nothing they won't do and I'd never forgive myself for putting him in harm's way.

I take my tea into my bedroom and consider whether or not enough time has passed for me to reach out to my sisters. I wonder whether Nadia found the note in her bookshelf. It'd be so nice to send a single email to my sisters telling them that I'm alive and well. But it's still too soon. I sit at my desk and... *that's odd.*

My senses heighten and not in the magical, Caleb's touching every part of me pre-sex sort of way. My computer isn't where I left it. I always keep it closed in the top drawer of my desk. But it isn't there.

Somehow, it moved. I'd never leave my computer on the end table by my bed. I once read an article about electronics being too close to you at night being the cause of all sorts of cancer. It scared me and since that moment, I haven't done it.

*So why is my computer on my bedside table? It wouldn't have been Caleb. He avoids technology like the plague and he's the only person who has been here besides me.*

I walk toward the computer with caution. This time I know I'm not being paranoid. Someone else moved this, there's no doubt about that. But maybe there's a chance it was Caleb, though I couldn't see why or when he would've taken it out of my desk drawer.

My heart rate ticks up and I take the laptop back to my desk and plug it in. I open the screen to find that I've been logged out and all of my suspicions are confirmed. Someone else has been on my computer. I haven't logged out of this thing in months.

*These are the kind of subtle mind games Doss used to play all the time. But is it possible that it was him? Could he have found me?* My throat runs dry.

I swallow back my fear and walk through the rest of the cottage looking for evidence if an intruder. Only, nothing looks out of place. Someone broke into my cottage, got into my computer, but didn't take anything.

Every sign points to Doss or the Red Dirt Brotherhood MC. But what can I do about it? Should I move again? Call the police only to find out they have connections to the club and reveal my location? Should I get in contact with my sisters just to make sure they're okay? I can't, surely the club has tapped their phones.

I think I might be sick. I pace the room as my walls come closing in around me. An hour later, I'm still wracking my brain, only now I'm doing it in the greenhouse. I need a project to occupy my mind at least until Caleb gets off and I can talk this through with him.

Throwing myself into the task of unburying the overgrown clay pots that sit out front of the greenhouse seems like as good a choice as any. Now I'm covered in hose water and splattered mud when the sound of footsteps crunching the pine needles on the ground has me jumping out of my skin.

"Hey," A man's voice makes my blood run cold and when I turn, I see Hank Hemlock grinning at me.

I blow out a deep breath. "Shit. Mr. Hemlock, you scared me. What are you doing here?" Caleb's words of caution run through my mind.

He smiles at me and I take a step backward keeping one hand on the hose. "I've just gotten back from town, and I wanted to let you know the place is buzzing with your name. That usually happens when new people move in, but you've managed to be somewhat of a ghost since you arrived. You can imagine how surprised I was when I realized that they were all talking about *you*. The girl I dropped off at my old cottage."

"Is that right?" I shake my head. This isn't a great time to hear town gossip, but I take the bait. "What could I possibly have done? I'm just here, working in the greenhouse and fixing all the little death traps you left me in this cottage. I don't bother anyone."

"There's someone looking for you. The search has been going on for a full day now from what I hear. They can't be stopped..." He lets out a breathy chuckle that makes my blood run cold.

He keeps talking, but I can hardly hear him over the sound of my own heart thudding in my ears. I swallow hard and try to keep my face from pinching into tight lines. This isn't the time to show how afraid I am. I take a deep breath as he rambles.

When I speak, I keep my voice calm and measured. "Mr. Hemlock, I need you to think back and give me as much information as possible. Who is the man looking for me? Did he give a name? What did he look like? Was he driving a motorcycle?"

The old man throws up his hands in a too casual gesture. "How the hell do I know? Didn't see him myself. I heard it over at Lumberjills Bakery. No need to work yourself up into a tizzy over it. It's all par for the course in Lumberjack Lagoon. And from what I heard it isn't a man at all. It's a woman. But who knows. What I do know is that they don't know where you live. I kept that to myself when they asked me. Figured there must be a reason you're hiding all the way out here and I wasn't gonna be the one to give you up."

The forest spins around me. "Thank you, I appreciate it. But I've really got to get going."

Mr. Hemlock keeps talking as he turns to start back up the gravel drive. I take the opportunity to dart into the cottage and lock the door behind me.

# 8
# caleb

When I arrive at Ariella's cottage after work, it's obvious something is off. I can see it in the way she moves before she even utters a single word. She's jumpy, she's pacing, and when I step in through the doorway, she's quick to lock the door behind me. This is beyond her usual nervous energy and her concern puts me on high alert.

"What is it?" My voice is a low, threatening growl. I'm already seething. I don't bother to take my boots off just in case I need to step outside and take care of whatever or whoever has her so worked up.

"It's just that..." Ariella hesitates. She looks up at me, then chews on her bottom lip. Tears well behind her eyes and it sends rage coursing through me.

No one, and I mean no one makes this woman cry on my watch.

"What happened?" This time my words have more edge than I mean them to, but I don't hold back.

Ariella walks past me and looks out of her back window. "Someone is looking for me in town. It's for sure now. Mr. Hemlock came by and told me today while I was outside in the greenhouse. I didn't want you to get mixed up with the guys from the Red Dirt MC and now they're probably here."

"I thought I told you to stay away from Hemlock. He isn't a good dude."

She shakes her head. "I was out back and didn't hear him coming, but that isn't the point. This is so much bigger than some creepy old man. Someone is here. Someone found me all the way in Lumberjack Lagoon. There's a rumor that it's a woman, at least that's what he claimed. But what if that isn't right? What if it's Doss? Or it could be a woman and she could still be connected to the club. Things like that happen all the time. This person, whoever it is, made it all the way to Lumberjack Lagoon from Texas. It won't take long to find me now, not the way the gossip flies in this place." The words rip from her throat with such force it breaks my heart.

But I exhale. Rumors in Lumberjack Lagoon are a dime a dozen. My chest lightens and I take a seat on the wooden bench beside her front door, untying my boots. "That's okay sweetheart, even if this person finds you, it won't be the end of the world. We have no idea who it is, maybe it's someone wanting to sell you more books. It could be a tea peddler here to find his ideal customer. Whoever it is will have to come through me. I had a good time protecting you the other night. I could do that again." I let out a chuckle.

Ariella crosses her arms. "This isn't funny and it hasn't stopped with a single rumor. Someone was in here. In *my place* without me knowing. I don't know how they got in but it must've been while I was in town. The worst part is, they weren't looking to steal anything. The only thing touched was my computer."

I pull my boots off and put a hand to the taut muscles in the back of my neck, rolling my head from side to side. "I've got to hop in the shower, but you don't need to worry. It isn't anyone from a motorcycle gang. The computer thing was me, I wasn't going to tell you this yet. But now you've ruined the surprise. The person here to find you is probably your sister Nadia." I look over to her, waiting to see the smile spread across her face. A swell of pride builds in my chest.

"What are you talking about?" Her mouth drops open and then closes with a snap. "And how do you know my sister's name?" Ariella takes a half step back and cuts her eyes at me.

I have to admit, the look she's giving me isn't exactly the thanks I was expecting. With her eyebrows taut into a line and her mouth turned down, she looks more upset than excited. Maybe she didn't understand what I was saying.

I lean forward to clarify. "I saw how much it hurt you not to have your family close to you because of some asshole a world away. As much as I get annoyed with Kai and Cain, I don't know where I'd be without them in my life. So I found them for you. You deserve to have a full life and that includes your sisters. Eloise was harder, her social media is like Fort Knox. After looking at Roslyn's social media, I wasn't so sure. I figured Nadia was the one to reach out to. So—" I smile, feeling proud of myself when Ariella cuts me off.

"So you got into my computer, and you took it upon yourself to endanger their lives and blow the cover I've worked so hard to conceal. You found her. You found my sister who was never lost. I'm the one who disappeared." She presses her fingers to her temples like she can't believe what she's hearing.

It's like she honestly thinks I'm the one in the wrong here and it's mind blowing.

"I did get into your computer, but I'm not afraid of some douchebag showing up here on his motorcycle with his friends to hurt you. It ain't gonna happen sweetheart. If he did have the nerve to roll into my town of lumberjacks, we'd take care of it. Full stop. End of story." I furrow my eyebrows as I watch her grow from angry to livid. "Do you know how many lumberjacks are in this town?

We're a brotherhood too, and we don't need the dumbass jackets or bikes to prove it."

Her arms fold across her chest tightly and then unfold so she can point accusingly at me. "You had no right. You don't understand the kind of people you're dealing with. You don't know what it's like to live in a town where they are above the law and you sure as hell don't know anything about the lengths I've gone to in my life to keep my sisters safe. How arrogant do you have to be to think that you can step in and override the decisions I make for my own life?"

Now it's my turn to stand with my jaw dropped in shock. "What the hell are you talking about? I'm not trying to override anything. I know you love your sisters and I wanted to make that happen for you. You wouldn't have given me their information, I already tried that. You didn't even want to tell me their names."

"Right, then you took it anyway." The words come out almost under her breath and it's hard to tell whether or not she's even talking to me. "Another man, taking control of my life. I ignored a million red flags last time, and look where it got me. I'm hiding all alone halfway across the country... I can't do this again.... Caleb, you have to leave."

Anger whips through me, tightening the muscles in my jaw. *How did this go so terribly wrong?*

"What the hell are you talking about? Don't you compare me to him, that's not fair. I know how to treat a woman and I didn't do this to hurt you. I did this to—"

"But It wasn't your place. Isn't your place." There isn't any bite left to her words, only sadness and it breaks my heart. "Look, I appreciate all the help you've given me. But you need to know that you're way out of line here. I told myself I'd never let another man come in and control me. We're only a few weeks into this thing, whatever it is, and you're looking through my computer. You're stepping in and taking over. Now there's a chance that you lead him straight to me. Once a fire is lit in Doss, he won't stop. If he thinks Nadia has information, the club will come for her too. They could be watching her phone, her social media, there isn't anywhere safe." She puts a hand over her mouth at the thought.

I take a step toward her and place a hand on her lower back. "Listen, sweetheart, I'm not going to let anything happen to you or to Nadia."

Her head snaps up toward me. "How can you promise me that? You aren't there, you don't know what it's like there. Bad men have resources and are above the law... and you can't be here either, not right now. I think I fell in too deep too fast and I can't let that happen. I'm sorry Caleb, but you need to go. I will figure this out."

The last of my sadness and shock melts away. It swirls together turning into a molten heat that courses through me, burning my stomach and pulling tension in every muscle I have. "Okay, then I'll go."

*I'll go find this asshole Doss Blakely, and when I do, there will be hell to pay.* I pick up my phone and dial my cousin Asher Oakes. The two of us are in my truck and on the road within the hour.

# 9
# ariella

I'm so upset when Caleb drives off that heaves of sadness wrack my whole body. But I didn't give him any other choice, what did I expect him to do? Sit in his truck out front all night like some sort of stalker from a motorcycle club? Of course not. He's so much better than that.

I hate that I'm stuck in a vicious circle of not being able to trust my own judgment. Caleb hasn't shown me a single red flag since I've known. At least he hadn't until today. But when he did, he went hard.

Caleb going through my computer and reaching out to Nadia is a violation of trust that has potentially ruined everything I've been working toward. It's going to take me a while to process through the implications of his actions.

On one hand, I know Caleb was genuinely trying to help me. That's all he's ever done since I met him. In a perfect world, I'd have my sisters safe with me right here in Lumberjack Lagoon. Maybe someday we can work toward that, but for now the less they know about me, the better.

On the other hand, Caleb has no idea what he's done. Both me and Nadia are in danger now because he couldn't leave well enough alone. Chills run across me when I realize that I've sent my only protector away.

It'd be nice to have someone to call to help me process all of these big emotions. What if the person looking for me *was* actually Nadia? What if I could call her? She's my best friend; my little sister who's always seemed so much wiser than me. I'd tell her everything and together we'd figure out exactly what to do.

An hour later, I'm sitting with sheets tacked up in my windows and my back to the front door. I've got to make a plan for how I can move forward. Only, I can't. Right now, I'm paralyzed by fear and regret. I don't know who to trust and I can't tell what stings more, sending Caleb away or disappearing off the face of the earth when it comes to my sisters.

*Tap. Tap. Tap.*

Three quiet knocks on my front door have me scrambling to my feet and my heart leaping into my throat. *Dammit.* I look around for a weapon and come up short.

I fly down the hall and into the bedroom. I pull my pepper spray from the nightstand as the light knocking repeats in a pattern. *I'm so thankful Caleb replaced the locks.* On my way back to the door, I pick up a frying pan from the kitchen. I'll go Rapunzel on his ass if I have to.

I take a deep breath and unlock the deadbolt keeping the chain lock engaged. When I crack the door open I can't believe my eyes. It's Nadia. I have to blink back my shock a few times just to be sure because the sight of one of my favorite people standing at my door is too good to be true.

I rip the door open and crumble into her arms. My sister and I embrace for what feels like a lifetime. When I think better of it, I pull her inside, locking the door behind us. “What are you doing here?” I blink back tears of joy.

“What the hell is wrong with you? I thought you were dead. I thought he finally took it too far and those stupid Red Dirt Brothers of his covered it up.” Tears stream down her cheeks. “Eloise and Roslyn were worried sick too. We can't lose another sibling. The last few weeks took me right back to when we lost Nicholas. I still think they have something to do with his accident and it wasn't hard to imagine them doing the same to you.” Nadia cries and it breaks my heart.

Tears wash my cheeks too. “I'm so sorry, I was wrong. I thought it'd be better without me there. I thought that the only way any of us would have a peaceful life would be for me to disappear. So that's what I was trying to do. I left you a note on your bookshelf telling you that I'd be back after enough time had passed.”

“I haven't done a whole lot of reading since my big sister dropped off the face of the planet.” She rolls her eyes. “Thank god Caleb called me. Imagine my surprise when some massive lumberjack FaceTimed me and gave me directions to your place. I mean the man's not bad to look at, but give me a break. Turn left at the third oak tree, round a bend, and make a right at the water tower. What the hell is this place? I had to go into town and ask around just to figure it out...” The ghost of a smile plays on her lips as she continues her rant, and I exhale.

She's mad, and she has every right to be. But she's here and that is everything. A slow growing confidence crawls over me. I know we're going to be okay.

“Caleb was right, you deserved to know. I'm so sorry and I promise you I won't ever disappear again. I was just worried about what Doss and his brotherhood would do to you if he thought you knew anything about where I was. Oh my god, I don't know how I messed this up so badly. I have so much to apologize to Caleb for and so much to tell you."

"Start at the beginning," Nadia says.

---

In the next two hours, Nadia and I sit at the tiny kitchen table Caleb made for me. We catch up on all things running away, the new cottage, and of course the lumberjacks. I tell her about Hank Hemlock and my dream of turning the greenhouse into a bookshop. We talk about Caleb and the way he's captured my heart.

Nadia tells me that she lost her job as an administrative assistant because she isn't cut out for corporate life. I tell her that isn't a surprise. None of the Astor women are made to work in a traditional setting, we've got too many big ideas to be climbing someone else's ladder.

As we talk, I exhale for the first time since I discovered my computer was moved. It's clear that bringing Nadia here is a step in the right direction and I can't wait to call Caleb and fix things with him.

Letting my bad memories of my relationship with Doss taint my chance at finding true love with Caleb is stupid. I need to apologize to the man who has brought so much comfort to my new world.

Nadia and I take turns erupting into fits of laughter when something stops me in my tracks. Through the thin sheet I tacked on the kitchen window, I see distinct movement behind the house. I can't make it out exactly, but the shape is large enough to be human.

I spring to my feet. "Shit."

"Shh, I see it too," Nadia says. She moves toward the light switch and flips it into the off position.

"What the hell is it?" I whisper.

"I guess I hope it's a bear at this point. We should call the cops.

Wait, are there even cops to call out here or is it just a bunch of lumberjacks with chainsaws who show up?"

I drop my voice to a whisper. "Lumberjacks from what I can tell, but I haven't had to test the theory yet." I reach for my phone and unlock it, getting ready to dial 9-1-1.

*Ding-dong.*

Before I can put the call through, the doorbell rings followed by four sharp taps that make my blood run cold.

"Hey Arilella, it's Kai. Let me in."

I blow out a deep breath and my shoulders sag with relief when I hear Kai's familiar, warm voice through the door. "Oh thank god."

"Do you know him?" Nadia asks, her eyes still wild.

"Yes." I rip the door open, Nadia stands behind me eyeing him with caution.

"Hey." Kai blocks out the light in the doorway with his imposing frame. But the big, charming grin on his face is disarming.

I hear Nadia exhale and her voice is a whisper too. "Holy shit, do all the men in Lumberjack Lagoon look like that?"

"Hey, you scared us. This is my sister, Nadia," I tell him. "What are you doing here?"

"Nadia, it's nice to meet you. I'm Kai." Kai's eyes rest on Nadia for a moment too long before he returns his attention to me. "Caleb left town, he had uh... something to take care of. But he said you were worried about staying safe. He wanted to make sure you had time to talk to your sister. I'm here to tell you that you sure as hell will be talking tonight. My cousin Beckett Oakes is out back, you might see him in the shadows, but he'll keep himself scarce."

Another man steps forward with his hand outstretched. "Hi, Garrison Staller. I'm the Lumberjack Lagoon Sheriff, it's nice to meet you. We've been researching the man who's been giving y'all so much trouble and I can see why you're worried. There are a lot of skeletons in those Red Dirt Brother MC closets. We've made arrangements for your younger sisters... Roslyn and Eloise, is it?"

My heart rate ticks up. "Yes, that's correct."

"What about them?" Nadia asks.

Garrison continues, "We've put in a few phone calls to have them watched by a private security detail until things settle. As for the two of you, tomorrow morning you'll be heading for a small cottage on the backside of the Oakes family property. You'll be safe there for a week or so and totally undisturbed while we get to the bottom of Doss Blakely. Any questions?" Sheriff Staller is so authoritative and direct that it doesn't leave any room for questioning a single thing out of his mouth.

"No, I guess not." I blink back my shock and Nadia furrows her eyebrows in my direction.

The idea of Doss not being able to interfere in my life or my sister's lives anymore sounds too good to be true. I hope the good guys know what they're dealing with. But right now, I can't come up with any explicit words of caution. All I feel is a surge of relief that leaves me so tired I can hardly wait to fall into bed.

"This is unreal, so they are lumberjacks with guns. Didn't expect that. Crazy." Nadia mumbles to herself.

Kai puts a hand on the inside of my doorway. "You ladies sleep easy tonight, we aren't going anywhere. We're posted up. We're on special orders from Caleb to stay out of your hair, so that's what we're going to do. But we'll be here if you need us. Pack your bags as soon as you get up."

"Do you know when he's coming back?" I can't help but ask.

"Caleb's working on a project. It will be at least a week or so," Kai says.

"It's just odd, he didn't mention any projects," I say.

"Well, this one just came up. Don't worry about him, he knows what he's doing." With that, Kai says goodnight to us and takes a seat in the rocking chair on my front porch.

When the door closes, both Nadia and I are stunned into silence. We stare at each other for a long while, but I break first.

"I can't believe Caleb's done all this for me. He didn't have to, I was so rude to him. I asked him to leave. What an incredible man… I wonder where he is… What do we do now?"

Nadia raises her eyebrows at me. "When a man like that tells you to pack your bag, you pack your bag."

# 10
# caleb

It's been over a week since we left. When Asher and I get back into town, I'm exhausted. But I've only got one chance to make things right with Ariella. It took me a lifetime to find her and I'm not going to lose her now. Knowing she's tucked away on the Oakes family property is a comfort and I've got one more thing to cross off my list before I bring her home.

Even if Ariella's done with me, and I hate the thought, I need Ariella to know that she's safe in Lumberjack Lagoon. It would devastate me to see her with another man, but I'm not that asshole ex of hers. I wouldn't stop her. I would keep loving her from afar and I would make sure that no one ever bothers her again. So I get to work.

I don't tell her I'm back. Instead, I call everyone I know with a tractor. I sound the alarm at Timber Logging and cash in every favor I have. The guys rally for me just like I knew they would. Kai, Garrison, and my cousins Adler and Beckett Oakes lead the charge without me having to ask. They show up, organize teams, and execute my plan with military precision.

From there it's another week of sleepless nights, but she's worth it. Another week passes by the time I'm ready to pick her up from the Oakes cottage and take her to her place. I'm running on fumes. I send word of my arrival to Ariella through my cousin Jules who lives on the property near the cottage.

Kai tells me that he wants to pick up Nadia himself. He claims he wants to give me time with Ariella, but I'm not an idiot. I don't buy that bullshit for a minute. But it's in my best interest to have some alone time with Ariella, so I take him up on it without calling him out.

When I pull up, I don't know what to expect. She's probably mad as hell and I don't blame her. I locked her away for weeks like some kind of Disney princess in a tower. I'm ready to apologize. I'm ready to do and say anything it takes to keep her in my life. But as soon as I stop the truck, my fears dissipate.

Ariella rushes out of the front door toward me with a massive smile on her face. "You're here! I'm so happy you're here. I've missed you. You look tired." She raises up and plants a sweet kiss on my lips.

"I am tired, but I'm here and that kiss was a much better greeting than I expected." I plant a kiss on the top of her head and she pulls away to look up at me. "Hey, sweetheart."

"I'm sorry I overreacted and I'm even more sorry that I didn't trust you. I know you weren't trying to control me and now thanks to all you've done, I've got one of my sister's here." In a single movement, she throws her arms around me and buries her face into my chest.

I hold her so tight I can feel her heartbeat. When she tells me that I'm her favorite person, I relax into her touch.

I inhale the sweet floral scent of her hair. "I missed you and I'm sorry if I overstepped. When I realized how much your family meant to you, I couldn't stand the thought of some asshole keeping you away from them. When I found out just how big of an asshole I was dealing with, I had to take action. But that's all behind us now. Let's just say he won't be able to bother you for a very long time."

"You went to find Doss? You shouldn't have done that. He's not a good person. He can be so dangerous and I would never have told you to go." Her eyes widen and she looks up at me from beneath her long, dark, lashes. "Wait... What does that mean when you say he won't be able to bother me? You killed him?"

A humorless chuckle rips from my throat. "I said I'm a bad guy, but not that bad, damn. No, I didn't kill him. That's motorcycle club shit and I'm a lumberjack. But the dude's in jail where he belongs and for a long time too."

Her eyes well with tears and a smile plays at the corner of her lips. "You're kidding. With all his money and connections, I never thought it was possible."

"It took some work. But I brought all the files from your computer with me. Garrison's got some friends in the District Attorney's office and they contacted the folks over in Findlay. It was too big of a case with too much hard evidence to ignore. Plus, they've been looking to bring down the big players in the Red Dirt Brotherhood for a while. I'm not saying those other boys weren't mad, but they aren't coming here. I can promise you that."

"You are incredible." She closes her eyes and when she opens them I can feel the weight lift off her shoulders.

"Oh, and I think I know why your car wouldn't start. He put something in the gas tank, it was all right there on the camera footage. Stalking, threatening, and breaking into your house. He followed you, your sisters, the whole deal." I swallow hard and debate telling her this last part but she deserves to hear it. "There's even some evidence that suggests what happened to your brother wasn't a total accident. He was mixed up with some bad people and it looks like Nicholas had more enemies than you thought. They're looking into that too."

She takes a sharp inhale of breath. "Wow. I always suspected he might have something to do with Nicholas, but Doss made me feel like I was crazy for even bringing it up. What a bastard." Ariella presses her eyes closed and I take her hands in mine.

"Whatever the truth is, at least we will know. It will be uncovered and people will have to take responsibility for what they've done. But you were smart to get away from them, they are into some dark shit. The good news is, Doss won't be out for a long time either way. I made him a personal promise to be waiting for him when and if he does see the light of day again. I couldn't help myself." I let go of a self-indulgent smile at the memory of Doss Blakely's face when I surprised him with a swat team on his way home from his club. He didn't much like the tables being turned on him and I didn't miss the opportunity to point it out.

Ariella's eyes flutter closed as she falls back into my arms. "You claim you aren't a good guy, and maybe you aren't perfect all the time. But you're one hell of a man. I love you, Caleb Greenwood. Thank you for being in my world.."

I open the door for her and Ariella climbs into my truck.

Before I shut it behind her, I make one last promise. "I want you to know that I'm not going to control you. I'm not gonna follow you or make you dependent on me. I want you to stay by my side forever. But if that doesn't happen, you are still safe here in Lumberjack Lagoon and I'm ready to prove it. Let me take you home."

# 11
# ariella

When we step in through the front door of my cottage, it looks like home, only different. The door itself is the same pink-blush that I painted it, but it's got more heft to it now. When I look closer I realize, this isn't the same door at all. I tap on it and note the solid rumble.

Caleb's voice comes from behind me. "This is a steel reinforced door. You can't kick through it, believe me, Kai tried. He wanted to test out the warranty before we got it installed. Your windows are shatterproof and the tint lets you see out without letting people see in. You get all the view and all the privacy too. This place is officially your fortress. Whether I'm here or not, and I plan on being here, you are safe."

I smile up at him. "I can't believe you did this. Caleb, this is incredible and so thoughtful."

I wander through the cottage and stop in front of a new bookshelf that stretches floor to ceiling. All my favorites are crowded onto it and it's a beautiful sight.

"Nadia told me to organize them by the color of the rainbow which was a pain in the ass." He lets out a grumpy chuckle.

"That sounds like her," I laugh.

My eyes roam the shelves, but when I find a framed picture of all five of the Astor siblings from a few years back, including Nicholas, it stops me. It's been awhile since I've seen his smile looking back at me. The sight brings a tear to my eye.

I pick up the photo and run my fingers across it. I can feel Nicholas almost as if he was here. There's a bond between the oldest sibling and the youngest that can't be broken. We certainly had that in life, and I'd like to think we have it in death too.

As I stare at the photo, Caleb comes to stand behind me. He places a protective hand on my shoulder and I'm overwhelmed with gratitude for the incredible man in my life. *This is what love is supposed to feel like, I'm sure of it.*

"Nadia forwarded me the pictures. No more looking through your computer, ever. That's a promise." His breath is hot in my ear and I turn to face him.

"You are the most incredible man. Thank you for this."

"I'm glad you like it sweetheart, but I've got to be honest. This isn't what I wanted to show you." He bites back a grin that lights the tired shadows under his eyes. "Come on out here with me."

Caleb takes me by the hand and walks me around to the greenhouse. When it comes into sight, my jaw hits the floor. The approach leading to the front door is unrecognizable. The plants are still here, but now they form a whimsical path to the entrance complete with overhead string lights that illuminate our steps.

The cobble stone path is stable and wide. When I walk in through the new oak doors, the sight in front of me takes my breath away. I can't believe my eyes. The inside of the greenhouse is unrecognizable. The walls are lined with rows of handcrafted oak bookcases stained a dark, warm, wood color.

I run my fingers across the smooth surfaces. "Did you make these?"

"Yeah, we had a bunch of old growth timber laying around the yard at work. I took a planer to it and they shaped right up. I had some help from a few friends and family too." One side of Caleb's mouth pulls up into a sexy smile that drives me wild.

An old record player plays new Beyonce and my worlds collide. "I can't believe this. Caleb, this is amazing! You are amazing!"

The shelves are overflowing with books of every size and genre. The stacks are only interrupted by the variety of potted plants tucked in amongst them that add to the warmth and charm of my little bookshop.

In the center of the room beside the register there is a vintage tea table. It's adorned with all the necessary items for a proper tea ceremony including glass cups, a kettle, and a tiered tray ready to be filled with my homemade scones.

At the back of the room is a vintage mustard-yellow couch opposite an armchair stuffed with bright cushions. In between them, there's a lamp on an end table. On the floor beside it is a massive dog bed for Buck. It's the perfect little cozy reading nook I can already imagine families gathering around and making memories.

My eyes rake across the room catching new details with each pass. I can't believe what Caleb's created. This man knows me more than anyone ever has and I'm so grateful for the life we're going to create together here in Lumberjack Lagoon. This bookshop is my wildest dream made real, just like Caleb.

Tears spill from my eyes as I wrap my arms around his waist and bury my face in his chest. "Thank you. I love you so much."

"I love you sweetheart." Caleb plants a kiss on the top of my head. "Your website is up too. You are officially ready for customers. But I can admit I didn't have anything to do with that one. My buddy Garrison had to help me out. Either way, it's all yours. Welcome to your hideaway at Lumberjack Lagoon."

# 12
# epilogue: nadia

***Three Months Later***

Life is beautiful in Lumberjack Lagoon. Caleb and I got married right away. The ceremony was perfectly simple and held right here in front of the greenhouse. It was just the two of us, plus our siblings and Buck, of course.

At first, we thought living in Caleb's more spacious place would suit us. His cabin is beautiful and modern after all. But in the end, I couldn't walk away from my charming little cottage. Caleb said that he could be happy anywhere as long as we're together.

I love the way Caleb made this place safe for me. But I have to think the over two-hundred-pounds of lumberjack who lives here is probably the best security a girl could ask for.

Now our tiny cottage is overflowing with flannels, lumberjack gear, and love. Caleb and I are so thrilled with each other and our little bookshop that every day feels like a honeymoon. We are a complete family unto ourselves, totally content to wake up, make love, spend time at the bookshop, and repeat. I never imagined a life like this, but I'm so grateful it's mine.

The Hideaway at Lumberjack Lagoon is officially up and running. It's quaint and charming. I make sure we have a ton of fresh florals that I cut from the forest around us everyday. I'm always surprised when locals make the journey all the way out here just to spend time walking the shelves and chit-chatting about the latest releases. But the bulk of our sales come from online purchases.

Roslyn and Eloise fell in love with Lumberjack Lagoon when they came out for the wedding, but not enough to stay put. At least not yet. Though I have a feeling that they could be convinced in the future. But I'm so grateful Nadia stayed in town.

She didn't stay for the bookshop, but while she's figuring out what she wants to do with her life, she's helping me pack and ship orders. She's thinking about opening some sort of dog grooming business, but that isn't what kept her here either.

In the end, Nadia couldn't shake the appeal of small town life in this stunning lagoon any more than I could. But secretly, I suspect the flirtation between her and my new brother-in-law also has something to do with it... maybe that's just wishful thinking.

*Bark. Bark.*

Today Nadia and I are busy packing up online book orders. There aren't any customers, but it feels busy here. Kai and Caleb are bustling around making a plan for Cain's triumphant return home before his final deployment.

*Ring. Ring.*

I look at Nadia, her arms are overflowing with books.

Then I reach for the phone. "Hideaway at Lumberjack Lagoon, how can I help you?"

A woman's voice comes on the line. "Yes, I'm looking for Miss. Ariella Astor."

"It's Ariella Greenwood now, but this is her."

"Ariella, my name is Frances O'Harris and I'm a social worker in Findlay, Texas. I'm calling about your brother, Nicholas Astor."

My heart sinks in my chest and I put the phone on speaker, shaking my head at Nadia. If this is some kind of cruel prank, just the mention of Nicholas' name has taken it too far.

I clear my throat. "I'm sorry, but this can't be about Nicholas. He passed away three years ago." I swallow hard.

The mention of my brother's name has Nadia and Kai's eyes trained on the phone. Caleb takes a step toward me, wrapping a protective arm around me.

The woman continues in a slow, calculated manner. "Correct, I see that here in the file. To be more specific, this call is about Nicholas' son, your nephew, Tate Astor."

My jaw drops open and my heart rate ticks up. "Who? Wait... what?"

Nadia leans over me. "Ma'am, hi, this is Nadia Astor. Our brother didn't have a son."

"I'm afraid that isn't correct. He's four and he's in my office now," Frances says, and I cover my mouth to hold in my shock. "He's entering the foster care system as his mother is unable to care for him. She's signed away her parental rights to the court. I'm contacting you as the next of kin. We need a suitable placement for Tate. If either of you think you might be fit for the position, we'd like to send an agent out to Lumberjack Lagoon and have a conversation."

My heart pounds in my chest and time stands still. *Nicholas has a son. A part of my brother is alive in this world and I had no idea. That little boy is entering foster care when he has a great big flock of aunts and a new uncle who loves him before we've even met him. This isn't right.*

*I don't want to be a mom. I never have. But do I really have a choice at this point? I can't let my nephew grow up never knowing his family, and who is his mother anyway? What's happening to her? It must be terrible, because no mother in this world voluntarily terminates parental rights unless it's bad and there aren't any other options.* The room starts to spin and my throat closes in on me.

France's voice is calm and measured. "Is that a conversation we can have or shall I call down the list? I see you have two additional sisters, Eloise and Roslyn, I—"

"No," I start, my voice wobbling. I won't let this burden fall on my sisters. I'm the oldest. I'm the only one with a house and a stable partner. I wish we had time to walk it through, but Caleb and I will figure it out. I take a deep breath. "I think—" I start, my voice wobbling with hesitation.

But Nadia cuts me off. "I'll do it." She blurts into the phone with the enthusiasm of a kid on Christmas. "Start the process, bring him today."

Nadia's eyes are wide and glassy from tears. But her mouth is turned up into an enormous grin. She's jaw dropped, fanning herself, and swiping at tears, but none of it can dull the smile.

"What?" I blink at her in shock.

"I'm pleased to hear that, but Ma'am we can't just send a kid across the country," Frances says. "We'll need to do a home study and make sure the living situation is suitable."

"That's no problem," Nadia says. "I'm sure you'll find my home quite suitable for children."

I cover the phone with my hand and drop my voice to a whisper. "You don't have a home, what are you doing?"

"Whatever I have to," the resolve in Nadia's voice makes me reach out and wrap an arm around her.

"I will help you every step of the way," I nod.

"Wonderful. We can start the paperwork now if you're available. Your full name please," Frances says.

"Nadia Victoria Astor."

Frances continues, "And your husband's name?"

"Um..." Nadia's face flushes red. Panic flares in her eyes. "I don't, um..."

Kai comes around the counter, clears his throat, and leans toward the phone. "Kai Greenwood."

# 13
# bonus scene: doss blakely

***Present Day***

You'd think these places would be cold, but in the dead middle of Texas, they just aren't. It's humid and I'm sweating through my prison blue shirt. My feet are pressed against the cement floor and my head is thrown back onto the mattress of my bottom bunk.

Time in the slammer isn't anything new for any of us guys in the Red Dirt MC. Still, a part of me can't believe that it's actually come to this. Unless I can pull some strings, it's going to be a long time before I see the light of day.

What's worse is that there is some douchebag lumberjack out there patting himself on the back for taking me down. Me being stuck in here isn't his victory to celebrate. That idiot is putting his nose in a world so complicated, he can't begin to understand it. No one from the outside gets the inner workings of the business, not like I do. I grew up in this life.

Simply put, my mom was a biker whore before she settled down and became Ace's old lady. It isn't a slur, Ma was born into this life too. Spent her time being happily passed around by the men who used to run this club. The first time I sat in on a meeting, I was still in diapers. I don't know who my father is and I learned early on it was best not to ask. Instead, they all raised me, the club is the only life I've ever known.

I was a quiet kid, I spent my childhood learning the rules, observing the patterns, and biding my time. By the time I was ten, I'd seen a lot of things I shouldn't have. I learned about loyalty, punishment, and the consequences of betrayal.

When I turned twelve I went through my own initiation into *the* life. It was a rocky start and they never expected me to rise the way I did. But with years of pent-up anger, there wasn't anything I wouldn't do. I always knew I'd land on top.

The guys in the brotherhood never saw me coming up through the ranks until it was too late. Now I have friends in high places; a judge here, a sheriff there. For a while, I was untouchable.

So no, a lumberjack did not put me here, I know exactly how I got here. I got comfortable. I started to think I was above the law and I let my guard down. A sloppy, stupid mistake has me locked up for months, but the outstanding warrants they have on me mean they could keep me for years. I'll get out and this stint will be just another notch of my belt. But what I will never fucking get over is how these women come into my world and take and take and never appreciate a single thing I do for them.

Take Ariella Astor, if anyone else is to blame for my being here, it's got to be that bitch. She drove me to this. When I met Ariella she was an innocent private school girl with no parents. Drove me wild. She thought I was wrong for her, but I was determined to make her my old lady no matter how long it took.

A carefully placed nail under the tire of her car while she worked a late shift led to an impeccable timed flat tire. When I swooped in to save the day, I introduced myself as the hero in her story. I knew exactly what to say because I had already done my homework.

I knew Ariella better than she knew herself. She was an eighteen-year-old, innocent, fatherless, private school girl with the weight of the world on her shoulders. I read her like a book and gave that girl everything I had. I knew where all of her buttons were and I pushed them relentlessly. She never saw me coming and fell for it hook, line, and sinker.

To her credit, Ariella resisted me at first. It took me longer than I thought it would to get her into my bed. We waited a full three months before I had that little girl's mouth wrapped around my dick and taught her exactly how to please me.

When she hated her job, I told her to leave it behind. When she refused, I made it happen for her. It only took one incident of a stolen item appearing in her bag for the shop's owner to let her go. Then when she couldn't afford her rent, I moved her in with me. She insisted on keeping her junker of a car, but I found a way around that too. There wasn't any reason for my girl to be slumming it. Not when I could give her everything she ever wanted.

In the early days, I told her how much I loved her. I told her that we were going to live life together and that she was to be the mother of my children as soon as possible. I thought she understood how good she had it.

I don't know a single woman who wouldn't love to have her every need attended to and Ariella fooled me into thinking she was the same as the others. She thanked me. She smiled and she was all too happy to turn a blind eye when I got wrapped up in shit she didn't care to know about. Ariella loved the perks of a life with me... until she didn't.

Out of nowhere, I went from being the man of her dreams to being the man she hid things from. I had my suspicions for a while, but they were confirmed one night while she was in the shower. I was completing my nightly inspection of her purse when I stumbled upon all the evidence I needed.

It turns out my little, sweet, Ariella was playing with fire. She'd taken it upon herself to get a prescription for birth control when she knew I wanted her knocked up. All those nights of filling her with my seed, it's no wonder nothing came of it. The fury burned through my body at the realization that she was capable of playing me for a fool. It made me wonder what else she'd been hiding.

When I questioned her, she told me that it was her body her choice or some other woke shit like that. I told her I'd forgive her, but that wasn't me. I really wish she would have stuck with my plan because that little pack of pills changed everything.

If she'd been secretly avoiding getting pregnant even though I told her I wanted a child, there was no telling what else she'd been up to. But I was hell-bent on finding out. I decided to play her game.

Ariella had so much freedom and she took advantage of it. But the joke was on her because that privilege was easy to take away. I needed to remind her who was in charge. That's when I started hiding cameras.

They served so many purposes, collateral, and surveillance. But most of all I liked the feeling of watching her. It was a victimless crime and there was no end to placement. I watched her in the bathroom and captured pictures of us in the bedroom. It's easy to be high and mighty when no one knows you like to take it in the ass.

She probably would have never caught on, but I lost my cool one day. She pissed me off by going to a doctor's appointment that I didn't approve of. So I printed the photos I'd captured in secret and displayed them on our kitchen countertop.

When she saw them her eyes went black with rage, the jig was up. Ariella was done playing nice. She tried to leave me right there on the spot, but I'm not a rookie and I couldn't have that. She belonged to me and besides, she knew too much.

The first time she left me, her plan was poorly executed. I knew a full week before she had the nerve to take action. I sat back and let her play out her little scheme. If she thought I wouldn't notice the missing cash, the stuffed duffle bag in the corner, or the burner phone. She was wrong.

When Ariella did go, I did what anyone would do. I let her leave and had my guys follow her in silence at a distance. If I'm being honest, what started out as a way to protect her, to keep her close, became something more. It was my reward, my obsession.

I still fantasize about it. I close my eyes and I can see myself standing outside her bedroom window at night in the shadows. Then I'm hiding in the corner of her work parking lot just long enough to lay a hand on the hood of her car and determine how long the engine had been off. I loved every part of it, standing statue still, hiding disguises in my bag to follow her all in my quest to save her from herself. It was... exhilarating.

But it wasn't just for sport. A novice would have stopped her from creating a new life outright, but that isn't how I do things. I needed to know who her allies were and what resources she was depending on. That way I could take them away one by one.

I wanted her to know that she was nothing without me, so I made sure she found out on her own. It wasn't a coincidence that she couldn't keep a job in the same way I was unsurprised to hear of her sister Eloise picking up an assault charge she didn't earn. Then there was her brother, god rest his soul, I made him one of us.

When everything in her life crumbled around her, Ariella had no choice but to come running back to me right on cue. I had her back where I wanted her, but it wasn't the same after that. She was more... opinionated.

She was willing to stand up to me on matters big and small.

There were eye rolls and I could feel the weight of untold secrets in the room. It was getting harder to keep her in line. Slowly but surely, I felt her pulling away from me.

The more she drifted, the tighter I held the leash. I went so far as to make up a threat from a rival gang. I had my boy Axel smash up my face to drive my point home.

*It's a dangerous world and you can't exist in it without me.*

Yet somehow, she did. When Ariella extracted herself from my world in the middle of the night, I was shocked. Hell, I was impressed and the chase was on. I checked in every corner of this godforsaken place, but she wasn't anywhere to be found. I had to hand it to her, Ariella managed to vanish.

Finding her became my full-time job. From day one, I knew her sisters were the key. She'd never leave them, at least not for good. So I shifted my focus to Nadia Astor and eventually, she led me right to Ariella's new front door. The ramshackle A-framed cottage was the biggest downgrade I've ever seen. It was unfathomable that she chose that over the life I could give her. I was dead set on bringing her back.

Of course, I had no way of anticipating the fact that Ariella recruited an army of lumberjacks of all things. I mean, what the fuck, we hardly have trees out here in Findlay. How could I have prepared for a damn vigilante lumberjack?

I underestimated those dudes from the beginning. They're bigger than I thought they'd be and I sure as hell didn't imagine they'd be smart enough to land me here. I'm not ready to move on because where I'm from you don't forgive and you sure as hell don't forget.

For now, I'm rotting away from behind these bars, biding my time, and plotting my revenge. But it isn't all bad. I've got a new lady in my life and this time, I know things will be different.

# pretending with the lumberjack

*Hideaway at the Lagoon Book Two*

# 14
# prologue: kai & nadia's meeting

I put my ear to the front door of Ariella's small A-frame cabin. My hand rests on the doorknob. There are muffled voices coming from inside, but when I ring the doorbell, they go silent.

I know that Ariella is home. She doesn't have anywhere else to go and Caleb has made sure that I don't either. She doesn't know it yet, but we are both here for the night. My brother seems to think she's in a dangerous situation. The only conflict I plan on facing tonight is figuring out where I'm going to grab food at this hour.

Still, when Ariella doesn't answer right away, the thought of some motorcycle gang looking for her makes me pound on the door with four more sharp knocks. I relax as soon as I hear footsteps coming from inside the house.

My brother cares about this girl, that much is obvious... and I can see it. Ariella is easy to like. Keeping her safe for a single night on Caleb's behalf shouldn't be too difficult. Not with the backup I've got with me.

Hushed whispers come from behind the door.

I clear my throat. "Hey Arilella, it's Kai. Let me in."

"Oh thank god." I can hear the relief in Ariella's voice as she fumbles with the locks.

"Do you know him?" Another voice chimes in, this one is unfamiliar.

"Yes." Ariella pulls her front door open.

I look at Ariella, her eyes are swollen and red. She's nervous and it infuriates me that some dude halfway across the country has her feeling this way. But I know my brother is more than capable of handling that. Ariella is safe in Lumberjack Lagoon and I'm going to do my best to make sure she understands that until Caleb gets back.

Then my eyes fall on the woman standing behind her and peering up at me. There's a similarity in the two women, both are tall with long hair and huge eyes. They are curvy in all the right places. *This must be the sister.*

But I can't help but notice that they are different too. There's a sweetness to Ariella, but her sister is hot as fuck. The woman oozes confidence and that is sexy as hell. I can't help myself. My eyes run up her thighs, across her massive tits, and land on her full lips. My heart rate ticks up and I run a hand through my hair. When our eyes meet, a hot electricity crackles between us. All I can think is that this night just got a whole lot more interesting.

I let my mouth fall into a massive grin and lean into the doorframe. "Hey."

The woman lowers her voice and leans in towards her sister. "Holy shit, do all the men in Lumberjack Lagoon look like that?"

She's going for subtlety, but I catch every word. *No fucking chance. This is all me, sweetheart.* I don't bother to bite back my chuckle. If she's impressed now, I only wish I'd taken off my shirt for this interaction.

"Hey, you scared us. This is my sister, Nadia." Ariella breaks the momentary spell I'm under. "What are you doing here?"

"Nadia, it's nice to meet you. I'm Kai." I like the way her name sounds on my tongue.

Ariella's crossed arms and impatient stare pull me back to the task at hand. She taps her foot impatiently.

I continue, "Caleb left town, he had uh… something to take care of. But he said you were worried about staying safe. He wanted to make sure you had time to talk to your sister. I'm here to tell you that you sure as hell will be talking tonight. My cousin Beckett Oakes is out back, you might see him in the shadows, but he'll keep himself scarce."

I hear Garrison on the gravel behind me and turn to shoot him a fierce, silent warning. *Don't talk to her, this one's mine.* I'm surprised at my own possessiveness, but there's something about Nadia that has me instantly entranced.

"Hi, Garrison Staller. I'm the Lumberjack Lagoon Sheriff, it's nice to meet you. We've been researching the man who's been giving y'all so much trouble and I can see why you're worried. There are a lot of skeletons in those Red Dirt Brother MC closets. We've made arrangements for your younger sisters… Roslyn and Eloise, is it?"

"Yes, that's correct," Ariella says.

"What about them?" Nadia asks. Her concern for her younger sisters is etched in the tight lines on her face and it makes me all the more intrigued.

Garrison continues, "We've put in a few phone calls to have them watched by a private security detail until things settle. As for the two of you, tomorrow morning you'll be heading for a small cottage on the backside of the Oakes family property. You'll be safe there for a week or so and totally undisturbed while we get to the bottom of Doss Blakely. Any questions?"

*Nadia is going to be in the cabin on the backside of our family's property for a few days. This is news to me... the best news. It's an opportunity I'm going to take full advantage of.*

"No, I guess not." Ariella stamors her response.

"This is unreal, so they are lumberjacks with guns. I didn't expect that. Crazy." Nadia furrows her eyebrows and mumbles to herself.

I put a hand on the inside of the doorway, subtly flexing until I see Nadia take notice. "You ladies sleep easy tonight, we aren't going anywhere. We're posted up. We're on special orders from Caleb to stay out of your hair, so that's what we're going to do. But we'll be here if you need us. Pack your bags as soon as you get up."

"Do you know when he's coming back?" Ariella asks.

"Caleb's working on a project. It will be at least a week or so." *Long enough for me to find out what Nadia looks like underneath that sweatshirt.*

"It's just odd, he didn't mention any projects." Ariella's lips purse into a tight line and it's reasonable.

But it's also on Caleb to handle that.

"Well, this one just came up. Don't worry about him, he knows what he's doing." I'm sure as hell not going to be the one who tells her that Caleb is off finding her ex-boyfriend and confronting his gang.

Ariella flashes me a look that tells me she knows I'm not telling her the whole truth. I take that as my cue to leave because she won't be happy when she finds out what's really going on. I wish her goodnight and take a step towards the big rocking chair on her front porch. Ariella mumbles a stunned *thank you* and steps inside of her house.

But before her front door closes, I reach for Nadia's hand. When I take it, sparks shoot up my arm and my breath catches in my throat. Nadia's eyes widen and her mouth parts in surprise, but she doesn't pull away from me. Instead, she stays perfectly still as she stares up at me and her hand fits in mine like a glove.

"I don't want you to worry about anything tonight. I've got you. Trust me." The corner of my mouth pulls into a smile.

She chews her bottom lip. "I do. I trust you."

# 15
# kai

My heart thuds in my chest at the feel of Nadia's hands under my shirt. The forest seems to quiet around us. She plants kisses on my stomach and her fingers dance along my zipper.

"Nadia, hold on. It's your turn." I back her against a tree and roam her curves.

She pulls away from me. "Kai, do you want me to check my calendar? I'm sure that it's your turn today. Now come on, it won't take too long for my sister to notice that I'm gone." She pulls me down and I sit on the stump of a massive tree we cut down at work last summer.

Nadia climbs on top of me and her lips press against mine. Her kiss leaves me breathless. Fire ignites between us and rages through every inch of my body. I'm going to miss this when I leave. The weight of her body on my lap has my heart thudding in my chest as she straddles me.

Nadia rocks forward, sandwiching my face between her massive tits and making me pulsate and ache for more. Our mouths collide again and our tongues intertwine in a frenzied dance. Electric sparks shoot through me and I give in to my hunger for her. If she wasn't so damned stubborn, maybe things could be different. Maybe this thing between us wouldn't be temporary.

The cool forest morning and the golden sunrise between the tree canopy disappear. Nadia is all I can see. She reaches between her legs and tugs my zipper down. I give up on trying to maintain my composure. I'm rock hard, my tip is slippery, and she knows exactly what to do.

Her slender fingers wrap around my throbbing length. She pumps with a fiery intensity that sears through me. I thrust into her touch. The rhythmic motion is like a shock wave to my core. Pleasure courses through me and I'm already aching for release.

She slides backward off my lap and drops to her knees in front of me. She spreads my thighs and my breath catches in my throat. This isn't the first time, sneaking off with my new sister-in-law, and my body trembles in anticipation of what's coming.

Her tongue glides down the length of my throbbing shaft, sending shivers of pleasure whipping through me. Nadia looks up at me as she curls her lips around the head of my member. A low groan rips out of me as her warm mouth engulfs me entirely.

She moves her head back and forth, taking me deeper and deeper into the depths of her throat until I hit the back. Nadia hollows her cheeks and it sends me over the edge. My hands instinctively find their way to the back of her head.

Her tongue dances along my girth. She teases me, lingering along the underside of my length. I steady myself from the overwhelming sensations coursing through me, but it's no use. Nadia's every touch consumes me.

As pressure builds in me, I grip a fistful of hair and tug her head to exactly where I need it. I thrust into her mouth desperate for more friction and she gives it to me. With a final bob of her head, my muscles clench and strain. I explode in white-hot bliss and Nadia milks me to the last drop.

I'm left panting, my shoulders thrown back and my chest heaving while Nadia gets to her feet. She brushes the forest floor off the knees of her jeans and I zip up my pants.

"You are incredible." I try to pull her close, but Nadia shrugs away from me. "Hey, I need to tell you something. I'm—"

"Stop it." She cuts me off.

I haven't told Nadia about my move yet. She doesn't know about the apprenticeship or the new life I've worked so hard to create for myself. But there's a part of me that doesn't want to. I don't know whether I'm worried about upsetting her or worried that she won't care at all. Either way, when she cuts me off, I let her.

Her mouth pulls sideways into a smile and she places a hand on her hip. "You can't start looking at me like that if this is going to keep working. Same time next week, right? My turn."

"Yeah, same time." I drop an arm over her shoulder and settle for planting a kiss on the top of her forehead. "But you'll see me later this morning at the bookshop. I've got to meet my brother."

"Can't wait."

# 16
# nadia

I pull the packing slip for the order in front of me and search for the books on our shelves. *The Maid, Things We Hide from the Light,* and *Bath Haus*… I'm pretty sure whoever ordered this could be my new best friend.

Reading has always been my escape. But I never imagined I would work at a bookshop in a tiny lumberjacking town. Especially not one that my sister owns. Hell, I never thought I'd leave our hometown.

If I had to guess I'd have said that by now I'd be a mom and a housewife married to a rancher on some farm. But now I'm a long way from the flat open prairies of Findlay and I've never been happier. Life is funny that way.

*Ding. Ding.*

The bell on the door chimes and when I look up, my heart flutters in my chest. Kai Greenwood makes a dramatic entrance, not that he has much of a choice. For starters, he's got Buck, the world's most adorable dog, bounding in behind him. On top of that, the man is striking.

He's a massive six foot four inches tall with the muscles of a professional running back. His golden skin is tanned by the sun and his chiseled jawline could cut glass. As much as I try to play it cool, my entire body melts at the sight of him.

I don't blame myself for the swooning. I imagine every woman he comes into contact with feels this way. The fact that I had his dick in my mouth a few short hours ago is technically my fault. But I let myself off the hook for that too on account of being in a sex drought for so long before I moved. Besides, no one else knows about it, so it's like it isn't even happening.

"What's up, Nadia?" Kai's eyes rake up and down my body pulling goosebumps from my arms and a stubborn smile across my lips.

"Good morning." I look up at him through long, dark, lashes not giving anything away. There are worse things than being greeted by a handsome and charming lumberjack this early in the morning.

"Brought you a coffee from Lumberjills, white mocha, extra whip, topped with cacao nibs, and a perfect one-hundred-three degree so it would still be hot by the time I got here."

*Ugh, this man is already irresistible, and now he has coffee too.* Kai hands the paper cup to me and his fingers linger on mine for a half second too long sending zaps of electricity whipping up and down my body.

"Thank you." I pull my hand away from his and look at my sister, Ariella, out of the corner of my eye.

Kai follows my line of sight and projects his voice. "You haven't changed your mind on that whole, *I'm an independent woman this year* thing, have you? Because I haven't changed my mind about wanting to take you on a date."

*And I haven't changed my mind about wanting to lick this coffee off your bare chest but you don't hear me shouting that across this bookshop.*

"If anyone could break me, it'd be you. But moving here is my official Eat, Pray, Love moment and I promised myself and my sister three-hundred-sixty-five days of dating me. I'm committed." *There's only three-hundred-twenty-one left, but who's counting?*

"If that isn't the worst thing I've heard all day." A smile tugs at the corners of Kai's full lips.

I let out a soft giggle and remember the tingle of his mouth on mine. The old me would have jumped head first into Kai's massive lumberjacking arms, but the new wiser me is holding space for myself. There will be no more jumping from one relationship to the next.

"Did you come all the way down here to shower me with gifts of coffee or are you looking for a new book?"

"He's looking for my husband." Ariella makes her way towards us.

"I'm right here." Caleb pops his head out of the back office. His voice takes on his typically sarcastic tone. "Our little brother Cain's heading home from his final deployment and this guy thinks we should buy balloons or some shit."

"Party planner of the year right there." Kai chuckles as he and Caleb head for the table in the back of the bookshop.

Ariella picks up a packing slip and we work side by side. We couldn't be more opposite, but it's easy to see how she fell in love with living here. This bookshop is her lifelong dream come true. It's her baby.

She's never wanted the kind you can hold in your arms or the white picket fence that goes with it. Caleb is the perfect man for her and I couldn't be happier that the two of them found each other. Ariella has sacrificed so much for me over the years, she deserves this happily ever after. Maybe I can find mine here too.

*Ring. Ring.*

# 17
# nadia

*Ring. Ring.*

I glance at the phone with a half-packed box spilling out of my arms. Then I look at the brass wall clock above it. It's too early for customers to be calling. It's probably going to be another heavy breathing then hang-up call if I had to guess. I head for the phone behind the counter.

Since Ariella left her nightmare of an ex in Findlay, his motorcycle club hasn't missed an opportunity to harass us. It isn't all on Ariella, I've dated a few of the Red Dirt MC brothers too. It was back before I knew better.

Before I left town they were a real concern. They kept tabs on all of us Astor siblings, showing up at our work and driving past our houses. But I haven't worried about it so much since I moved. With the pack of lumberjacks assembled around us out here, Doss and his gang haven't exactly been an issue.

*Ring. Ring.*

Ariella gets to the phone before I do. "Hideaway at Lumberjack

Lagoon, how can I help you?... It's Ariella Greenwood now, but this is her." Her eyes widen.

I don't miss the way her tone changes and the faint shake of her head. I stare at her watching the subtle changes in her face as she takes the call.

Ariella puts the phone on speaker. "I'm sorry, but this can't be about Nicholas. He passed away three years ago."

Our brother Nicholas' name has me fumbling my books and flying to my sister's side. Doss and his crew have pulled some low blows before, but this is too far. Bringing our brother into whatever this is hits below the belt. Caleb and Kai seem to get it too without my having to say a word. Now all four of us stand in silence, eyes locked on the phone.

The woman on the other line continues in a slow, calculated manner. "Correct, I see that here in the file. To be more specific, this call is about Nicholas' son, your nephew, Tate Astor."

My heart thuds in my chest and I feel dizzy. *What is she talking about? Our brother didn't have a son. He was never given that opportunity because he died too young.* Every muscle in my body tenses.

Ariella blinks, her face washing with a deep crimson. "Who? Wait... what?" She presses a hand to her temple and squeezes her eyes shut.

This is enough. Bringing Nicholas into this and making up a child is cruel. I won't have it. I lean over Ariella, speaking directly into the phone with a tight, clipped tone. "Ma'am, hi. This is Nadia Astor. Our brother didn't have a son."

The woman's voice is kind and gentle. "I'm afraid that isn't correct. Nadia, my name is Frances and I'm a social worker here in Findlay. Tate is four and he's in my office now. He is entering the foster care system as his mother is unable to care for him. She's signed away her parental rights to the court. I'm contacting you as the next of kin. We need a suitable placement for Tate. If either of you think you might be fit for the position, we'd like to send an agent out to Lumberjack Lagoon and have a conversation."

This knocks the wind out of me. *So it's real. This isn't a cruel prank. Nicholas has a son and he's sitting in a foster care office right now.* I'm too stunned to speak. I can't even see straight.

The room swirls around me and I'm overwhelmed with an intense shockwave of pure joy. *We might have lost Nicholas, but now some stranger is calling to offer us a part of him back into our lives. It's too good to be true.* I'm overwhelmed with an urge to find my nephew, wrap my arms around him, and hold on tight to the last living part of my brother.

France's voice is calm and measured and the sound snaps me back to the present. "Is that a conversation we can have or shall I call down the list? I see you have two additional sisters, Eloise and Roslyn, I—"

"No," Ariella starts, her voice breaking at the end.

My eyes whip to hers. My throat is too dry to communicate all the thoughts whipping back and forth between us. I know parenthood isn't a life Ariella's ever wanted for herself. She just settled into her happily ever after. She gave up her own childhood to raise me and our siblings. But even more than that, I know with everything in me, that little boy is meant to be mine. I can do this. I can give him a life that my brother should've. I don't know what Tate has gone through, but I know I love him.

Ariella inhales into the phone. Her face is drained and colorless and she presses her eyes shut. "I think—"

"I'll do it." I cut her off, my voice vibrating with pure joy. "Start the process, bring him today."

Tears of joy blur my vision. I can't help the enormous grin that stretches across my face. My emotions bubble to surface but I've never been more sure of anything in my life.

"What?" Ariella blinks at me, her jaw falling open.

Frances continues, "I'm pleased to hear that, but Ma'am we can't just send a kid across the country. We'll need to do a home study and make sure the living situation is suitable."

My heart stops for a beat and my throat runs dry. "That's no problem. I'm sure you'll find my home quite suitable for children."

Ariella covers the phone with her hand. Her words hiss out through clenched teeth. "You don't have a home! What are you doing?"

I inhale. "Whatever I have to."

This has to work. It took a million tiny events to bring my nephew to me and I know in my heart that this is the life I was meant to live. Having a piece of our brother back. Being a mother. Being able to hold our family together. It's everything I've ever wanted being dangled in front of me and I'm not going to let it be ripped away.

"Are you sure?" Ariella squeezes my hand and I nod. "Caleb and I will help you every step of the way."

Frances' voice breaks through my concentration. "Wonderful. We can start the paperwork now if you're available. Your full name please."

My head spins from the whiplash of it all. "Nadia Victoria Astor."

Frances continues, "And your husband's name?"

*My husband? Do I need a husband to do this? What year is this? Does not being married make me unfit? No. For sure, no. But what about the fact that I currently live on an air mattress on Ariella's living room floor? That's going to be problematic.*

Panic washes over me. I don't want to mess this up. Not when everything I've ever wanted is suddenly within reach. Not when my nephew might be entering the foster care system.

I falter. "Um... I don't, um..." I swallow hard and my vision blurs again. When it comes back into focus, I lock eyes with Kai.

Without a single word, he dashes around the counter and leans over me, speaking directly into the phone. “Kai Greenwood.”

# 18
# kai

I grab a rubber band from the cash register and take Nadia's hand. Her eyes are as wide as saucers when she turns to look up at me.

She lowers her voice to a hiss. "What the hell are you doing?"

I pull her hand back toward me and wrap the rubber band around her left finger. "You need a ring. We should do this for real. We should get married."

"What?" Ariella's mouth falls open. She speaks into the phone. "Frances, can you give us a moment, please? We're going to put you on hold for just a moment while we talk logistics. Thanks."

I feel the daggers my brother is shooting at me, but I ignore them. The only person in this room who matters is Nadia. When her eyes meet mine they are wild and unsure. But I'm not. I stare back at her with all the confidence in the world. All of my plans pale in comparison to the prospect of a life and a family with Nadia. If she won't marry me, at least I can sleep at night knowing I helped her get where she was going.

Nadia's words come out through clenched teeth. "Kai, what are you doing? No. No, I don't need you to do this. I am capable on my own. I will figure it out."

"I know you can, but I don't want you to have to. That will make an already difficult situation that much harder. Come on, think about it. We make a great team." I run a charm offensive, pulling out my most smoldering smile. From the way her face is scrunched together, I'd say it gets me absolutely nowhere.

Naida presses a hand to her temple. "Under normal circumstances, I'd be melting into an absolute puddle with that smile, but this isn't the time to be coming undone for a lumberjack who while hot is also apparently insane. We don't even know each other. What are we going to do, pretend to be married?"

"Yes. That's exactly what we do."

Nadia turns to Ariella. "Help me out here?"

Ariella twists a strand of hair between her fingers. "Well, you do live on an air mattress in my living room. That might not paint the best picture of stability. Maybe you let him do it, just for a while."

Nadia's jaw falls open. "What a traitor! Has everyone lost their minds? You want me to run around pretending to be engaged to a lumberjack I hardly know when I am a grown woman. We're losing focus, people. This little boy is our nephew and I know in my heart that I was meant to be his mother.."

"So we'll do this for him." I take the phone from Ariella. "It's settled. Nadia, we're settled, right? We have to be on the same page if we're going to pull this off."

"Okay," is all she says.

I clear my throat. When I speak on the phone, I don't leave any room for doubt. "Hello, Maam, thank you for waiting. My name is Kai Greenwood and Nadia and I are getting married. It's already in the books… We can't wait to welcome our nephew. Please move forward with the process. Let us know what we need to do and we will have everything ready on our end."

Nadia opens her mouth, but no words come out. Then she covers it with her hand and I wonder what she's holding in. The rest of the conversation passes in a blur as my new reality encroaches in around me.

I know I should be worried, but instead a sense of calm washes over me. In a single phone call, I've become a fiance and maybe even a father. I was made for this. All my life, I've tried to find a path that felt like mine but nothing has ever made sense until I met Nadia.

When we hang up, Nadia puts a hand to her chest and leans against the bookcase behind the counter. I put a protective arm around her and she doesn't push me away. Instead, my chest swells when I feel her fall into the comfort of my arms.

Ariella stares at us in stunned silence. I see a flicker of recognition in her eyes and I wonder if she can see all that exists between Nadia and me. For a few moments, the four of us stand in the quiet of our new reality. The only sound is the chattering of the forest outside.

There isn't any going back now. There won't be a move or an apprenticeship. Nadia won't get her year of independence. We're in this now, the four of us plus one little boy until death do us part. The faces looking back at me are in varying states of disbelief but this new reality fits me like an old hat.

Finally, my brother breaks the ice. "Kai, what the actual fuck was that."

"Leave it Caleb to say the quiet part out loud," Nadia mumbles under her breath as she pulls away from me.

Caleb folds his arms across his chest. "With all the work you've done, when your life is just about to take a turn… really? This is just like you. How many times are you going to get burned before you stop handing out matches."

"Caleb that's enough." My tone sharpens and I narrow my eyes at him. “I’m not you, thank fucking goodness. I know where my priorities are and I’m acting accordingly.”

“What’s he talking about?” Nadia looks back and forth between us.

“Caleb, enough,” Ariella puts a hand on Caleb’s chest. “This isn’t up to you.”

“It sure as hell isn’t.” Caleb turns and heads for the door without another word.

“Caleb, I know what I’m doing I’m not—” Before I can finish my thought, Nadia is whipping around to face me.

“It isn’t Caleb’s fault. He’s right. He’s the only one keeping a level head about this insane situation. I could’ve figured it out and you could have stuck to your real life. This is supposed to be my year of being an independent woman dammit and now instead we’re supposed to be married and we hardly know each other. Then there’s a little boy who doesn’t even know he has this huge family.” I see the tears build behind her eyes.

“Stop it. All of that was before we knew we had a nephew.” Ariella says. “Besides, we don’t know anything about Tate or what he's been through. He’s going to need support from all of us. This changes everything. How could it not? Thank you, Kai. Now I’m going to find that stubborn husband of mine.”

# 19
# kai

When it's just Nadia and I left in the bookshop, I put my hands on her arms and turn her to face me.

"Ariella is wrong. Not everything has changed. I've wanted to make your dreams come true from the moment we met. That will always stay the same. Now I have a chance to do that. It isn't exactly the way I pictured a proposal would happen, but I need you to trust me when I tell you, we can do this. You don't have to love me or stay married to me for a lifetime. But we can get your nephew here."

The words hurt as they come out of my mouth, but I mean them. I want the world for Nadia, even if I don't get to be a part of it in the long run. Fire bubbles on my skin where we touch. My chest tightens as I wait for Nadia to decide my fate.

I wish she would stop fighting me. I wish she could see that together we make so much sense. Finally, her eyes meet mine. I see the answer before she says it and I exhale. Nadia shakes her head, but I don't miss the way her mouth pulls up at the corner ever so slightly. I see an unmistakable flush of understanding passing over her face.

"Thank you for being willing to do this. It'd just be long enough to get the placement settled. Once little Tate is here, we can go back to our real lives, right?"

I squeeze her arms and bite back my smile. "Tate is going to be our real life. But we will take it one day at a time. I'm here and I'm not going anywhere until you tell me to."

She chews her bottom lip. "There are so many things I need to know about you if anyone's going to believe we're engaged. I haven't even seen your place. But I already know it's probably better than my mattress on the floor."

"You're going to come over to my place as soon as you leave here and I promise you we will make it all make sense. Can we start there?"

Nadia takes a long inhale. "Yeah, we can do that."

---

I scramble back to my place with just enough time to unpack a few of the moving boxes. If earlier wasn't the time to bring up my impending move, now certainly isn't any better. I've invited Nadia over before, but she's always refused, preferring our secret rendezvous in the forest.

A part of me doesn't believe she's actually going to show up until I hear the tires of Nadia's old Ford Focus crunching up the path toward me. My place still looks like an abandoned shell of a cabin, but it's as good as it's going to be on this short notice.

I open the door before she can knock and Buck bounds out to greet her. Once he gets his pets from Nadia, I push him aside and pull Nadia into my arms. "Welcome home, sweetie."

Nadia looks stunning, as usual. When she pulls away, she holds up her left hand. When I see the rubber band knotted around her ring finger, I can't help but smile.

"I thought it was fitting for my first visit to our place." She lets out a giggle and I usher her inside. Nadia's eyes widen as they wash over the cabin. "Kai no one is going to believe a woman lives here. In fact, I don't believe that anyone lives here. Are you some kind of minimalism crusader? I mean, where is everything? If it wasn't for Buck's water bowl, I'd swear you were just moving in."

I clear my throat. "Well, what did you expect from a lifelong bachelor, lumberjack-chic? I swear since they renovated that damn lodge in town, everything's gone buffalo-check."

Nadia lets out a long, breathy exhale. "Ha, you have a point. I guess we won't have to fight for space."

"No, we won't. There's a second bedroom down the hall, it's all yours. I'll get you a bed and whatever else you need. This goes without saying, but I hope you'll just share mine." I raise an eyebrow and see her face flush red at the offer.

"Kai, I think we need to take a break from our little hobby. This isn't the time to complicate things."

"You don't want to complicate our fake marriage by having real sex… got it." I let out a chuckle. "Come on, I'll give you a tour."

# 20
# nadia

"I wish my sister were here for this," I call down the hall to Kai. "Who goes on a second honeymoon anyway? They've only been married for three months."

"Why, that means my dumbass brother would be here too and that's the last thing we need today."

"Good point." My stomach clenches and I do one last walk through the cabin. It's only been two weeks since I first stepped foot in here, but it feels like a lifetime. The house itself is unrecognizable. For someone with a tendency toward minimalism, he sure has turned this place into a grand millennial dream.

The white walls are now rich and moody blues and greens. The bare windows are covered with cascading floor-length drapes in gauzy chiffon. The moving boxes that were draped with a tablecloth have been unpacked, finally, and replaced with an actual table. Kai has been the best sport throughout the process.

It isn't just the place that's changed. The sex has faded away between us after I made the request to uncomplicate things. *Do I hate myself for it? Yes. Sometimes. Of course. But was it the right choice? Also yes. Probably. Not sure.*

Though I don't like it, abstinence has somehow made us grow closer. It amazes me the way I've come to depend on him. The man is unflappable in the face of hanging curtains, personal space invasion, and not to mention becoming a fake husband. He's somehow struck a balance between giving me space and making me feel the most secure I've ever been.

Best of all, we've worked together to create the cutest little bedroom for Tate. We spent hours researching the interests of four-year-old boys and the room I'm staying in is fit for a Spiderman-loving, book-reading, lego-playing enthusiast.

"Sweetie, you've got to sit. You're going to burn a hole through that carpet." Kai comes into the living room wearing a button down and I almost forgot how nicely he cleans up.

"I know, I'm just nervous." I look out of the window and Buck comes to stand beside me. She isn't here yet. I scroll through my phone. "Okay, pop quiz." I hold up a photo of my sisters on my phone. "Who are these good-looking ladies?"

Kai examines the pictures. "Those are your younger sisters, Eloise the writer, and… Roslyn who plans on marrying for money."

"Hey!"

"What? You know I'm right. Never met her, but from what you and Ariella say…" He lets out a too-casual chuckle. "Come on, relax. We will be fine. We're completely believable as a couple. This place looks amazing and she'd be crazy not to let us have little Tater over here." Kai squeezes my hand and I find that I believe him.

"You're right. Okay, one more. Give me a quiz."

Kai rolls his eyes. "Who's my best friend?"

"Easy, Garrison, Lumberjack Lagoon sheriff."

*Ding Dong.*

I hop to my feet. "It's Frances, she's here."

"Before I forget, I got you something. It isn't real, but Ariella told me this would be a nice placeholder." Kai pulls a ring out of his pocket and slips it on my finger. Then he takes a step toward me, puts a hand on the back of my head, and kisses me. His mouth sizzles on mine and my body aches for him. When he pulls away, I stare up at him weak in my knees.

"What was that?"

Kai winks at me. "It's show time." He opens the door. "Frances, hi. Welcome to our home."

Frances comes inside. She's older than I thought she'd be, but she's petite and her body is rock solid. She's stunning without a single swipe of mascara, though she doesn't smile much. There's a real muscle-hamster vibe to her and I'm officially intimidated.

Kai on the other hand doesn't miss a beat.

Before I can think of a single thing to say, he's giving her a tour of our home. Then he tells her a clever story about how we met that has nothing to do with being almost related and having sex in a forest. It's pure lumberjack magic.

Every word out of his mouth is charming Frances, it's written all over her face. But he's charming me too. I'm so grateful to Kai for using his superpowers for good and I feel my heart swell for this man who adores me.

Thanks to Kai's ability to win her over, the home study is off to a fabulous start. An hour after her arrival, Frances feels more like an old friend than a caseworker. She's a Texas native, who instantly fell in love with the forest in our backyard.

That was all the prompting Kai needed. He didn't waste any time taking her out back and showing her how to chop wood. With those massive muscles, she took to the task like a fish to water.

Somewhere between wood chopping and her complimenting my scones, I decide I like Frances. But as we move to the kitchen table to talk business, I can only hope that she likes me too.

Once we're settled in around the kitchen table and I've offered her every beverage under the sun, Frances pulls out her computer.

Frances looks at us over the screen of her laptop as she types. "I shouldn't have an opinion on this, but between me and you, I hope this works out. You are a lovely couple, you have a wedding date on the calendar, and from the sound of it, you've got an excellent support system in place. Little Tate is such a sweet kid. I think it's a wonderful fit."

"Thank you." I glance at Kai and he gives me a reassuring nod, putting his hand over mine.

She continues, "I'm going to need an official statement from you to present to the judge about your plans for the future. It doesn't have to be lengthy, just an idea of where you see your life in a few years."

"Of course. My plan is to get married and be the best mom. I want to keep working for my sister down at the bookshop and give Tate everything." I ignore the fact that this plan is built on a house of lies.

Frances nods along as she types. "Okay, and you Kai. What are your plans?"

"Oh, my plans have changed. I thought I was on a path. But now that Nadia's here I want her to be happy. I want to see her become the mother she's always dreamed of being. I want to take care of my little family."

"Very sweet. Thank you, I'll get this typed up for you."

She isn't wrong. Kai is incredibly sweet, still, a flicker of discomfort passes through me. I wonder what path Kai was on before all of this chaos erupted in front of him.

"So you'll get this wrapped up and we'll have our guy here before you know it then?" Kai's enthusiasm is contagious and I can't help but smile at the thought.

Frances hesitates. "I'm afraid it isn't that simple. Just between us, the placement has been contested by a member of the mother's family. I shouldn't tell you this, but off record, the man petitioning for custody is the child's maternal uncle. Biologically he's got just as many rights to claim Tate as you do. But he's also got strong ties to a motorcycle club. If you can put together a package that showcases your long history of stability, custody is a shoo-in. But they're putting a lot of money behind this, so we have to be careful not to count your chickens before they hatch as they say."

"They don't say that here, I feel like that is very Texas..." Kai mumbles.

My heart sinks. "Is it..." I swallow hard. "Doss? He's in prison, I can't imagine it could be him but..."

"Doss... No, the name is Harvey."

"Harvey." *That son of a bitch.* I think I might be sick. It's Doss' right-hand man. Bile rises in my throat. My head swirls at the thought of my nephew being raised by those jackasses. "So Amber is the mother."

I want to call Ariella, only if I do, she'll talk to Caleb. The last thing I need is Caleb and Kai rounding up a bunch of lumberjacks to confront a motorcycle club. The walls of the room start to close in on me.

"Hey, we'll figure it out." Kai puts a firm hand on my thigh and squeezes.

Frances leans forward and drops her voice to a conspiratorial whisper. "I'm not worried. Let the judge hear your story. Show her pictures of your long history together and this thing will wrap itself up in no time."

"Right." Only we have no history.

# 21
# kai

When Frances leaves, Nadia and I sit at the table and talk things out until she is as pale as a ghost. We go rounds and rounds. But all the talking boils down to two heartbreaking questions from Nadia. *What if it doesn't work and how can I move on knowing that a part of my brother is living inside of that motorcycle club?*

She's spiraling and it's painful to watch. I've gotten to know Nadia so well in such a short time and Tate will be her whole world. That's exactly how I know that she won't be able to sleep unless I intervene. I open a bottle of red and pour her a glass. It takes some convincing but eventually, she has a glass. By the time the second glass is gone, Nadia can hardly keep her eyes open. I take her by the hand and walk her down the hall.

"Come on, there's nothing left for us to do tonight. We will work on this in the morning, but you did a brilliant job with Frances today." I pull back the sheet on Tate's bed and help Nadia in.

Nadia smiles up at me, her eyes glassy from the alcohol. "We both know that was all you. But even with all that charm I don't know if it was enough, I'm worried." She lays back against the pillow and I sit on the edge of her bed.

"I know you are, I am too." I plant a kiss on the back of her hand. "We will figure out a way to get him here. The judge will see it."

Nadia's eyes close and then shoot back open. Her words run together in an adorable slur. "I'm worried about something else too. I'm worried about you. What did you mean when you said you had other plans? Ariella gave up everything for me and I still feel the weight of that. I don't want to take anything from you."

"Ah, don't worry about that. I'd marry you tomorrow and not just because we want Tate here. I'd marry you forever and never look back." But by the time I finish my sentence, Nadia is already fast asleep.

For a minute, I keep my eyes trained on her. I take in the curve of her cheeks and the delicate features of her face. I notice the way her long eyelashes flutter as she drifts off. She is stunning. I want to give her the world because Nadia deserves it. Loving her makes me feel like the man I want to be. I'm desperate to make things right in her world.

When I'm sure she's asleep for the night, I close her door and get to work.

I start by making a call to my brother and interrupting his second honeymoon with the news of the Red Dirt Motorcycle Club's involvement in Tate's life. It takes everything in me not to drive down there and confront these assholes. But I can't make any moves against them with Frances and social services breathing down my neck.

The same can't be said for Caleb. Ever since the Astor sisters have come into our lives, Caleb's been looking for a reason to show them their place in this world. If the situation with Tate goes South,

Caleb is the contingency plan I'm not afraid to enact. But I hope it won't come to that.

The next few hours pass in the blink of an eye while I'm making lists, gathering supplies, and charging my camera. I don't sleep, but I don't care when there's so much at stake. I keep my head down and move as quickly as I can.

Before I know it, the sun is up and Nadia makes her way down the hall. She wearing a thin t-shirt with no bra that makes it fucking impossible to forget what her tits feel like on my lips. My body responds to the sight immediately, but I stay focused.

I get my camera ready and snap away as I sing, *"Happy birthday to you, happy birthday to you..."*

Nadia squints into the flash and then sits down at the table in front of the layered cake with an illuminated candle on the top. Her eyebrows furrow in confusion. "Kai, it isn't my birthday and what are you doing up at this hour? It's so early."

"Sweetheart, we're making history today. I know it isn't your birthday. It's not Christmas or Valentine's Day, it's not your graduation. But we're going to celebrate every last one of those events today and document it. We are going to paint a history so stable no judge can ignore it."

Her mouth pulls into a smile. "Kai, you're amazing."

I wrap my arms around her from behind and plant a kiss on her cheek. We hold the pose while I use my phone to take a birthday selfie.

"We're off to a great start. Now get dressed in your Christmas best sweetheart. The first thing we're doing is heading out back to trim our tree."

Nadia's hesitant smile melts away into a full-blown grin. "I can't wait."

From there, the day is a frenzied whirlwind. We cover all our bases and drive to every corner of Lumberjack Lagoon. Taking pictures where I look like a man in love is the most natural thing in the world.

We pose with coffee and winter hats at Lumberjill's coffee shop. We chase Buck up and down the slide at our local park. Nadia smiles and lets out a giggle when I catch her around the waist and pull her into my arms. We end our night with a romantic Valentine's dinner at Lumberjack Lodge complete with candlelight and off-season heart confetti.

We flip through the pictures on our phones and on my camera. Smiling back at us is a couple in love, that's impossible to fake. Even though I'm running on no sleep, I'm not tired. I'm buzzing with energy. Somehow, Nadia and I share a year's worth of memories in a single day and it leaves me aching for even more time with her. Nadia is without a doubt, my person. I start my truck to get us home.

"You did good, babe. I had so much fun with you today and we have a documented history that no one can contest." Nadia reaches across the center console and entwines my fingers with hers. "Thank you for being you. I couldn't do this with anyone else."

Her touch sends sparks whipping across up and down my arms. "Pretending to love you is the easiest thing I've ever done."

Nadia squeezes my hand. "What do you say we go home and make a night of it... Maybe we can take some pictures you can't send to a judge." She lets out a soft giggle.

"Hell yeah, that's a deal." My dick twitches at the thought of spending a whole night wrapped up with Nadia.

"Oh, Kai, can we make one last stop to get these printed? I want to put them together and get them mailed off as soon as possible. I promise to make it worth your time." She winks and I like where this is heading.

*One-hour photo, here we come.*

# 22
# nadia

Now my eyes open slowly and even though I'm awake, this still feels like a dream. Golden rays of sunlight filter in through the curtains and bathe Kai's skin in a warm glow. He's still asleep and I trace the outline of his massive arms.

Last night was somehow better than I imagined it would be. Kai and I devoured each other with an insatiable hunger, making up for lost time. My body is drawn to him like a magnet and the anticipation had me losing myself the moment we got through the front door.

This time there wasn't any talk of schedules or whose turn it was. Kai made everything about me. He took his time and peeled every article of clothing off me. Then Kai explored every inch of me with his tongue. I came alive under his touch.

When he couldn't take it anymore, our naked bodies entwined in a frenzy of passion that stretched on for hours. We spent the night locked in each other's fiery embrace. Even when we slept, our limbs were tangled and our hearts beat in perfect rhythm. I thought

I'd had every part of him in the forest, but now I understand that he was only getting started.

Kai's peaceful expression isn't disturbed by the sun being up. His steady breaths make my heart flutter with emotion as I replay every minute of last night in my mind. Being in his arms feels like the most natural thing in the world. He's almost too good to be true. But here I am, waking up in his bed.

A rush of adrenaline washes over me when I see the big manilla envelope on his desk. *The pictures, I can't wait to relive the day through pictures. I had no idea he had already taken the time to sort them. I wonder which ones he chose to send to the judge and whether they'll be enough to bring Tate into our lives.*

A surge of euphoria rushes through me as the realization hits that my wildest dreams are within reach. I pull Kai's button-down flannel shirt from the floor and slide it on. It smells woodsy, like him, and I breathe in deeply as I take a seat at his desk.

I run a finger along the folded seal of the envelope. Then I empty the contents onto his desktop. Before I get it open, I'm already grinning because I know what's coming. I'm ready to see yesterday in still shots, but this is something else entirely.

There are copies of Kai's driver's license, the results of a physical assessment and some kind of exam scored with ninety-four-percent at the top. This clearly isn't what I thought. I'm curious, but I remind myself that it probably isn't any of my business.

Kai isn't actually my husband. It shouldn't be a surprise, but somehow It's a bit of a shock when I think about it. I've been so selfish. Kai has had an entire life before me. This is clearly a holdover from that time in his life and an important one.

I slide the documents back into the envelope and wonder where in the world he put those pictures. But as my eyes swipe over the documents, I pause. I can't unsee the typed letter at the bottom of the stack of materials.

*Congratulations on your acceptance into our program.*

I scan further down. This is an acceptance letter for an apprenticeship and it's dated just a few weeks ago. A pit forms in my stomach. From there I can't help myself, I read it from top to bottom, pouring over every detail.

*Dear Kai Greenwood,*

*Congratulations on your acceptance into the lineman apprenticeship. Based on your exemplary test scores and exceptional pole climbing ability, we are pleased to offer you a spot in our residency program as well as a generous relocation bonus.*

*Please note that only the top two percent of applicants are accepted Into this prestigious program. You should be proud to find yourself among them. We are certain you will find a career with us that is unmatched.*

*Pack your things and prepare for a move in the next thirty days. Our relocation specialist will be reaching out to you with more information.*

*Sincerely,*

*Brain Chavez,*

*CEO, Brotherhood of Electrical Engineers*

My chest hollows out and then collapses in on itself. I ache with a deep emptiness that leaves me unable to breathe. No wonder his house was packed. I knew he wasn't a minimalism enthusiast!

Kai is putting off a once-in-a-lifetime opportunity for me. He's done all the hard work and he's succeeded. I won't let him give that up. The crushing burden of guilt engulfs me like a tidal wave, dragging me under until I'm suffocating.

This situation with Kai is like my sister all over again. Watching a person I love give up their life for mine is not something I'm prepared to do again. But back then I was a child and I didn't have a choice. Things are different now.

Bringing Tate into my life is my dream. This apprenticeship is

Kai's and I won't be the person who takes this from him. I take action immediately, springing to my feet and moving in silence collecting my belongings from his bedroom.

Kai is too sweet, too kind and he deserves to have everything he's ever wanted. I need to fix this, but I know him so well. He won't walk away from me and I love that about him. But it's time I let go of the fantasy of being a family and start acting on what's best for all of us, Kai included.

I pack most of my belongings and scribble a note. We can talk about this later, but after all he did for me yesterday, he deserves a little more peaceful sleep.

# 23
# kai

My arms reach out for her before my eyes open. I want to feel her warm curves against my hard lines. I don't know what time it is, but sleeping with Nadia's body tucked into mine soothes me like a missing piece to a puzzle that I didn't even know was gone.

My body is still buzzing with the lingering sensations from the most incredible night of sex I've ever experienced. Every touch, every kiss, every moan plays in my mind on repeat. I let my eyes close again and doze off with the memory.

It's another hour before I'm jolted awake by the realization of the empty space where Nadia should be lying next to me. But when my hands make their way over, her side of the bed is cold. I wonder how long she lay awake this morning waiting for me to get up. I wonder what time it is.

I get to my feet and head for the shower. The hot water rushes over me and I can't help but relive every minute of last night. I've never been so captivated by anyone. It is impossible to think when all the blood in my body is concentrated in my swollen member.

I squeeze and stroke, letting myself imagine the swell of her tits, the round of her mouth wrapped around my length, and the way her ass looked tilted up into the air. Nadia is all I'll ever need. It doesn't take me long to explode in white-hot bliss from the thought.

By the time I get dressed, I'm feeling better. I don't see the white piece of paper with my name written on it until I step into the kitchen. But when I do, it pulls a smile from my lips. There's no doubt that it's written in Nadia's perfect calligraphy. Normally surprising her is my thing, but there is an undeniable charm to waking up to a love letter.

I pour myself a cup of coffee and unfold the paper. But when I read it, my initial surprise quickly transforms into a deep sense of devastation.

*Kai,*

*I want you to know that I have fallen in love with you. You are an incredible man and you deserve the whole world. That's why I've made a decision. I want you to make your dreams come true. I saw your apprenticeship letter and you have to take it.*

*I'm going to take some time too. I'll be staying at Ariella's place for a few days while she's still gone. Let's respect each other by giving us some space to breathe. Please don't contact me. In fact, I'm going to turn my phone off.*

*Instead, get things in order to leave for your apprenticeship. I know it isn't too late to make your dream come true, I saw the date. I'm going to figure out what to tell Frances. I think I'll start with the truth, but I need time. Thank you for being my favorite person.*

*Xoxo, Nadia*

The weight on my chest feels like a concrete block. Each sentence pierces my heart with more intensity than the last. The room feels emptier than ever before, and my emotions swirl like a storm inside me. It's taken me all my life to find my place but I know for sure that it's right beside Nadia.

"Buck, your mom's lost her mind on us. She's left us with this terrible fucking plan, but at least she loves me."

Buck puts his head on my lap as I read the letter over and over until I come to a simple conclusion. *I'm not going to respect her space.* I tried that. We lived three months sneaking off to have sex in the woods when we could have been making a history that we didn't have to manufacture. I refuse to stand idle and watch the most incredible person slip away from my life I'm done with following Nadia's plans. It's time to go after my dream.

# 24
# nadia

The next seventy-two hours pass like molasses in January. I sleep as much as I can, which as it turns out, isn't much. I read three books cover to cover, and I exclusively eat bags of gummy candy. None of it helps.

I don't know what I'm going to tell Frances that won't make me look unstable and I sure as hell can't stop missing Kai. This is just like me, I jump headfirst into relationships then sink before I can learn to swim. The most ironic part is that I finally chose the right guy this time only to figure out that I actually am the problem.

But at least the timing of moving-gate has coincided with my sister and Caelb being out of town. I take advantage of the fact that their place is all but abandoned right now. In exchange for the hospitality they don't know they're providing me, I commit to spending extra time popping into the bookshop and packing up online orders to keep things running. It's just about the only productive thing I can do right now.

I walk out to the quaint bookshop behind Ariella's house and shove the creaky wooden doors. I tell myself I'm making the right choices, but I can't stop my shoulders from sagging with defeat and my eyes from burning with tears as I think back to the disappointment he must have felt as I selfishly ripped open his already-packed moving boxes. Of course, he could have mentioned that he was leaving to fulfill some lifelong goal, but I digress.

Ripping open another bag of sour gummy worms, I turn on Taylor Swift's *Folklore* on vinyl. I'm pretty sure I do feel something like an old cardigan, so it feels right. I throw myself into the online orders.

While I work, I squash down the searing pain that grips my chest and crushes my heart. My entire year of independence shatters into a million pieces as I sit here, reduced to a sniveling mess. Which is ironically the exact outcome I was trying to avoid.

*Ding.*

The bell chimes against the door as it flies open. Even though he's respecting a boundary I set, a part of me hopes it will be Kai ready to rush in and tell me he loves me all over again. But instead, I see a tanned and smiling Ariella rushing toward me.

*What the hell? What day is it? How long have I been under a blanket?*

"What happened? I saw the blankets on the couch and I know that look." Ariella comes for me with a big smile. She looks refreshed and glowy. I can only imagine what I look like in comparison.

"Nothing happened. What happened to you? You're back early."

She flips on the electric kettle. "Something um.. Something important came up. But why don't we start with why there's a massive stack of empty gummy worm wrappers scattered through the house."

"Well, it's because I didn't think you'd be home any time soon." I try to blow her off, but when Ariella tilts her head and crosses her arms, I fold. My trembling lips part and I tell her everything. I don't miss a single detail and I don't even try to stop the tears from falling as we talk.

Ariella pours each of us a cup of tea. "Why are you so devastated by the idea of him changing his dream to include you?"

"Because... that's what you had to do. You didn't get a choice. Mom and Dad died and you became a parent. I know what a sacrifice you made for me, Roslyn, and Eloise, even if they couldn't see it at the time, I did. I can't have another person I love making that kind of decision because of me."

Ariella's face pinches into tight lines. Then she comes around the corner, arms open. She wraps me in a massive hug. "Is that what you think? That breaks my heart. You are so... wrong."

"Wrong?" I let out a giggle through my tears.

Ariella pulls back and looks into my eyes, taking her hands in mine. "I never gave up my life for you, I had a life because of you, and I'd do it over a thousand times over. We didn't have parents anymore, my sisters were the only thing tying me to this world. I would've been so lost without you. Now you have a chance to be happy with an amazing man. Don't you dare let that stand in the way."

The knot over my chest loosens and I inhale for the first time since I saw Kai's acceptance letter.

"Do you think he feels the same way?"

Ariella swipes at her own tears. "Are you kidding me? Have you met the Greenwood men? They don't do anything they don't want to do. If Kai told you that he's made a decision to be involved in your life, then he's made a decision. The only thing standing in his way is... you."

"Now that sounds right. It's not the first time I've been my own problem. Ugh, I thought I'd outgrown this." I let out a humorless chuckle. "What the hell am I thinking? I need to fix things with him."

*Ding.*

The sound of the silver bell against the old door has me whipping my head up. My heartbeat picks up. *It's Kai. I already know it.* My breath catches in my throat and I get ready to throw my arms around his neck.

But my heart nearly stops altogether when I see Frances walk through the front door.

# 25
# nadia

I lower my voice. "Shit. This is the last thing I need right now."

"She's early," Ariella mumbles.

"Early? I didn't know we were expecting her at all."

"Don't worry, I've got this. Go wash your face." Ariella steps around the counter and rushes to greet Frances at the door. "Frances, hi..."

I step into the bathroom, taking the opportunity to collect myself. Checking the mirror I dab the blots of mascara from under my eyes and smooth my hair back into a ponytail. I don't need Frances seeing me in my hot-mess-express era. It isn't going to help my case. Plus, I need to talk to Kai before I put my foot in my mouth with Frances.

Thank goodness Ariella is back and on my side. When I make my way onto the bookshop floor. Ariella and Frances are chatting like old friends and sipping tea.

"Frances, hi. It's nice to see you again. Are you here for another interview or an inspection?"

Frances' eyebrows furrow and she tilts her head to one side. "No, not today. Of course not."

I put a hand on my hip. "So you flew all the way out to Lumberjack Lagoon for… another case?"

Frances looks at me like I'm insane. After a long pause she says, I'm here for your wedding. I thought it was so sweet of you to invite me and I had such a nice visit last time, I jumped at the opportunity to come again. I can't wait to take these photos of the ceremony back with me and include them in your file. Those Red Dirt MC guys don't stand a chance at taking little Tate."

My jaw falls open as I try to process what she's saying. I come up with a few options. Either Frances is batty and making things up or maybe I slept through some kind of alternate ending to my story with Kai. Somehow, Ariella doesn't seem to be confused at all which makes me think the latter is more likely.

*Ding.*

The bell chimes again, and this time it's Kai. The man is a sight for sore eyes. All I want to do is fall into his arms and tell him that if he moves, I'll move with him. With Frances' eyes on me, I keep myself together and calmly step around the counter toward him.

"Kai, good to see you. Look, Frances is here."

"Frances, hi." He steps toward her, wrapping her in a hug. She didn't strike me as a hugger, but she doesn't seem to mind it coming from Kai. "Thanks for coming."

Ariella gets to her feet. "I have an idea, why don't I take you to your seat and we'll let Nadia get ready."

"Absolutely." Frances holds out her arm and Ariella slips an elbow through it as they make their way toward the door.

*Okay, everyone has officially lost it.* I stand staring, my jaw hanging open in total shock.

Ariella turns back to look at me over her shoulder with glassy eyes. "Congratulations, I know this is going to be the best day of your life."

When it's just Kai and me, I look up at him, desperate to make things right. But before I can get in a single word, he puts his arms around me.

"I missed you and your plan sucks. So I came up with my own." He plants a kiss on the top of my head. "We're not going to solve anything by being half in. I love you Nadia and I'm doing exactly what you asked me to do. I'm making my dreams come true. You are my whole world. I'd give up everything if it means getting to love you day in and day out."

"I love you, Kai. You are too good to be true and I'm sorry I almost let my past get in the way of our future. I missed you so much. I don't want to be away from you, ever. I want to marry you, not just for Tate, but forever."

Kai's mouth lands on mine in a kiss that sizzles through my whole body. His hands lock around my waist and I feel him exhale.

"I'm glad you said that because there's a whole wedding waiting for us outside. Ariella helped me pull it together. She's got a dress for you too, it's in her closet. She said it will be obvious. I wanted to bring Frances into the magic of our love story because it's real. I get to marry you and it won't be just us, I get to be a dad to Tate, I know it. The only thing I can't figure out is how the hell a guy like me got so lucky. You are my favorite person, I'll meet you outside when you're ready."

---

As I emerge from the threshold holding a bouquet of wildflowers picked from the forest and wearing my white gown, I feel weightless. The air is filled with anticipation and the excitement is palpable. Twinkling lights dangle from the trees around us, casting an enchanted glow on the forest.

The entire Greenwood family is present and Kai's best friend Garrison is here too. When I see my sisters seated on rows of elegant gold chiavari chairs I smile through blurry eyes. This is a dream. It's too perfect to be real, yet here I am.

My eyes drift up the aisle to the man waiting for me. Kai is blinking back tears as his gaze locks on me. A sense of calm washes over me. I know without a doubt that I will love Kai forever. He's the man I've been searching for and now that we've found each other, I'm never letting go.

# 26
# epilogue: nadia

With trembling hands, I reach out and grasp Kai's fingers tightly. "Oh my gosh," I whisper, hardly able to contain my excitement. "Look, that's him. That has to be him." I can't believe this moment is finally happening. My entire body tingles with anticipation and I'm barely holding onto the emotions firing through me.

My heart pounds in my chest as I stare at the boy in the distance. There's something familiar about him. He's only five but Tate stands tall and proud, just like my brother did.

Frances comes back to her desk, she's hardly able to contain her smile. "Mr. and Mrs. Greenwood, it's my pleasure to introduce you to Tate. He's the coolest kid I've ever met and I'm thrilled that he'll be going home with you today."

Tate steps out from behind her and it's surreal. It's like looking into the past. There isn't any doubt that this little guy is an Astor. He's got the dark hair, the striking eyes, and the same deep-set dimples that my brother had. He looks up at me and time stands still. Every memory I have of my brother growing up floods back to me.

With a shaky breath, I hold out my hand to him. "It's nice to meet you, Tate. I'm really happy you're going to move in with us. I'm Nadia, your Dad was my little brother. "

"I know." He shoves his hands in his pockets.

My voice wobbles and I hold back all the things I want to say. *I'm sorry you've ended up here. You are loved. You are going to be okay in this world because we are going to make sure of it.* I can't imagine what he's been through.

"You know back home, we have a room all set up for you. I brought you some pictures of it, just in case you want to see them." I hand him my phone and he flips through the photos.

"That looks cool, so many trees there." The ghost of a smile plays on his lips and he pushes his hair away from his eyes. His arms fold tightly across his chest and when he sits in the chair next to Frances' desk, his shoulders sag.

"Tate, is there anything you want Nadia and Kai to know about you? Maybe you can tell them a little more about what you like to do or how you're so good in school."

Tate looks around the room and then inhales. "I just want to say thank you for, you know, wanting me to come with you."

The floodgates burst open. My heart breaks for what his little life must have held so far. "We want you so badly. I loved you from the moment I heard your name. I know it will take time, but I think that you'll find out we're pretty cool." I swallow my tears and Kai plants a kiss on the back of my hand.

"Yeah," Tate nods.

Frances opens a folder and lines the table with documents. Together they paint a clearer picture of Tate's past, but I can't keep my mind off the present. I want to know everything about this kid, but he shouldn't have to relive whatever is written on those pages.

"I, uh, I don't know if we should..." I start.

Frances looks at me, eyebrows arched. She may have missed my point entirely, but Kai gets it.

He leans forward with one eyebrow arched. “Hey Tate, I heard that you think you’re a pretty fast runner in your new shoes... I bet I can beat you.”

“He’s kidding. Tate, you’ll get to know us, he’s joking with you.” I clench my teeth and cut my eyes at Kai. “What are you—” I start, but then I stop when I see Tate’s posture change.

Tate bolts upright. “I’m super fast!” A slow-growing smile stretches across his face and the sight brings tears to my eyes.

Kai jumps to his feet and gives Tate a head nod. “Arc you ready to prove it or what? Let's get outside, it’s so boring in here. I’ll tell you what we’ll race and the winner gets ice cream before we head back to the airport.”

“Yeah,” Tate looks like a child for the first time since we met him. His eyes light up and he looks from Frances to me and back again, “Can I go?”

“Of course you can,” I say.

“We’ll leave you to it. We’ve got to figure out who's faster, right Tater?” Kai holds up his massive hand and Tate gives him a high-five.

Kai bounds out of the back door of the social services office with Tate trailing close behind. As I watch them walk, my heart explodes with joy. I don’t know whether it’s my imagination, but I swear that Tate copies Kai’s stride.

Frances steps away to grab another file and my phone vibrates in my pocket.

*Ariella: Can we come over to meet him yet?! Are you on the plane at least? What’s happening over there?*

*Me: All my dreams are coming true. You and Caleb will be the first to know when we touch down!*

*Ariella: Me, Caleb... and Eloise. She’s here.*

*Me: Holy shit.*

# how to lose a lumberjack in one date

Dear Reader,

*When Eloise Astor came into town at the same time Cain Greenwood was home from deployment, Ariella and Nadia cooked up a plan for a blind date between the two. But not every date can end happily ever after.*

*Nadia and Ariella had good intentions. They thought, "what if the third Greenwood brother and the third Astor sister became a thing? What if they got together only to find they couldn't resist each other? It would all be so magical!"*

*The blind date happened, but... spoiler alert Elosie and Cain weren't meant to be. Happily ever never landed between them.*

*Before you read Eloise's love story in Single Dad Lumberjack Hideaway at the Lagoon or Cain's love story in Captivated by the LumberJack, I think you need to experience the comedy of this blind date gone wrong.*

*Turn the page to read a bonus story right now!*

*Xoxo,*

*Elsie James*

# 27
# eloise astor

Ugh. If this dude looks at his phone one more time while I'm talking, I'm walking out of here. I don't even know exactly where *here* is, but I'm not a fan. This is some sort of adult Chuck-E-Cheese only designed especially for Lumberjacks.

I'm all for cheap beer and pool tables on a first date. But with the axe throwing and the buffalo check tablecloths, this place is on a whole new level. I finish off my beer, and then I clear my throat with extra emphasis. It's a not-so-subtle warning shot of sorts, and I hope my blind-date-lumberjack will take the hint. After all, Cain Greenwood isn't bad to look at.

Don't get me wrong, he's definitely got a lumberjack vibe... even his name screams *Man of the Forest*. But I suppose that comes with the territory. With his chiseled jawline and blinding smile, I could be convinced to climb him if the situation presented itself.

The waitress takes our order of mozzarella sticks for him and more beer for me. I don't miss the way she throws her hair back and bats her eyelashes at Cain. I can't help but think they might make a nice couple. I even find myself subconsciously wishing her luck, which isn't a great sign for him and me.

Cain doesn't seem to notice her at all. When she vanishes, he offers me a casual glance from over the top of his beer bottle. His phone is still in hand and that's all it takes for me to decide that I'm over it.

I throw in the towel right then and there, determined to call it as I see it. "So, you're back from deployment and already busy, huh? Lots of people to text right this minute it seems…" I trail off with a shake of my head.

Cain Greenwood meets my eyes for what can only be considered a half-second and nods. "Yeah, it's an old friend. Sorry, I just need a minute. I know this is rude, I wouldn't normally, but this is important. Let me step away… I'll be right back."

"You know what? I'm not worried about it, take all the time you need." I shrug and am surprised to find I really mean it.

I've never been someone who needs company. When that company is looking longingly at a text message, I'd much rather be alone. As soon as he leaves I finish my beer and then, I finish his too. Just like that, I'm feeling better about the night. Not better like *maybe Cain is the love of my life*, but better like, *I just noticed there are nachos on the menu.*

I get my phone out and stare at the blank notes app. Stupid writer's block still plagues me and that's not great when you write to pay the bills. By the time he makes it back inside, I still don't have any words down. But I do have a nice new buzz that takes the edge off. So I count it as a win.

Cain slides back into the booth. "Sorry about that."

I shrug with a laugh. "Don't worry about it. This is a weird setup, right? Basically, our siblings were like, *hey, you both have dead brothers so, you should go out.* And like, that's just not sexy." I bite back a laugh, but Cain doesn't follow suit.

Instead, his eyes widened. “Are you feeling okay?”

I sit up a bit straighter and reach for the water. “Yes, I’m fine.” And I am fine. I’m fine with this being a bad date. But I don’t need to get so sloppy he’s got to carry me out of here.

He softens, “But I do know what you mean. I can’t believe I’m doing this. A blind date isn’t my style. But I’ve been out of practice during deployment, so I guess they thought I could use some help.”

I let out a laugh. “Yeah, Ariella hit me with the, *come on we’ll be three sisters dating three brothers. It’ll be so cute.* But you know, cute isn’t my thing. I should’ve said no straight out of the gate.”

“Ouch.” A smile tugs at the corner of his mouth.

“I mean… no offense. The night is still young, maybe this will turn around for us.” My stomach sinks and I bite my tongue. “It’s just that I came here to work on my newest book, not to date anyone. I thought Lumberjack Lagoon would be a good backdrop for some inspiration.”

“Oh, so you write romance then?” He leans forward, interest finally piqued.

“No, I write thrillers actually. There’s lots of dead bodies and such.”

“Wow.” He gives an exaggerated nod. “Yeah, okay. I wonder what’s taking so long with those mozzarella sticks.”

# 28
# cain greenwood

The food arrives and we dig in. Thank fucking god the atmosphere lightens as I start to match Eloise drink for drink. But no matter how much I try to talk myself into this, something isn't working between us.

There are facts here that are hard to dispute. Eloise seems cool. She's hot, that's a given. Massive tits, which is a total plus. But I feel like I'd rather high-five her over a keg than bend her over a couch. With as long as it's been since I've been laid, that's really saying something.

I can't tell if it's the hard edge to her that's turning me off or the string of text messages that have my phone vibrating in my pocket. But either way, time is standing still on this date in the worst possible way.

I shake away my thoughts and try to get my head back in the game. "So tell me about yourself. We're technically family now, right? I should know *something* about you other than the fact you write horror stories for fun."

"Ah, there's nothing like a reminder that our family tree is looking more like a straight line these days. Should we take these shots first?"

"Absolutely." She throws hers back like a fucking pro and I'm impressed.

She might be the perfect woman, but for some reason, I can't make myself feel a single thing.

"So you aren't into scary books?" She teases me and her mouth pulls up at the corner, her words slurring at the ends just a little.

"I don't know, it's just that I've seen a lot of real-life horror since I've been enlisted. It makes it a little less fun to explore in my downtime."

*Fuck. I'm such a drag and I can't get out of my own way.*

"Right. Yes... Um, thank you for your service." She tucks a strand of hair behind her ear and stiffens.

I consider ordering another round, but a boy runs past our table. He's got a throwing axe in hand and I let out a laugh. "Only in Lumberjack Lagoon is a ten-year-old running past you with an axe, not a problem. You know I've always wanted kids. I think they have a way of lighting up a room. There's so much hope in them. What about you?"

Even buzzed I know that this has got to be safe territory. I mean, everyone likes kids, even if they don't have them or don't want them. Everyone has at least one amazing kid in their life.

She lets out a deep exhale and rolls her neck from side to side. "Yeah, kids aren't really my thing."

"Right, cool."

My phone buzzes in my pocket again. It's Gabby again, I know it. I know I should be paying attention to Eloise, but I can't not check the message. When my brother Kameron passed, he left behind too many things to count. But none as important as Gabby.

# 29
# eloise astor

By the time we've finished eating, we've both stopped trying altogether. But Cain is a gentleman and tells me that he's going to make sure I get an Uber ride home. He needs one too at this point.

The only problem is, there's apparently just one, solitary Uber driver in this godforsaken town. The dude is making his way back from the Portland airport. When I asked how long it'd be, Cain said it was impossible to know.

In lumberjack land, you don't use an app like the rest of America. You simply *text the dude*. He must not anticipate a ride anytime soon though because Cain decides that we should play a drinking game. Now that I'm matching him shot for shot, I'm liking him a whole lot better.

As the night wears on, the place goes from a lumberjack amusement park to a dive bar and I like it a whole lot more. I'm leaning against Cain to keep from falling over in an oversized booth back in a dark corner.

*Dammit, he's handsome.*

I run my nose up the side of his neck breathing in the warm smell of leather. When my eyes meet his, I smile. “Can I be honest with you? I wanted this to work so much. Because you’re fucking hot and your a lumberjack and a solider at that. You smell so good… But it’s a miss, isn’t it?”

He lets out a deep belly laugh. “It’s a fucking miss! I’m glad you said it.”

I can’t help but join in the laughter. “Okay, okay, I have an idea. Now we’re gonna have to see each other at every family thing from now on since we're technically, and not in a weird way, related.”

“True story.” He raises his glass in a toast to me.

“So let’s just try this to put the theory to bed once and for all. Are you in?”

“I’m so in Baby.” He growls, biting his bottom lip, and winks at me.

He’s smooth. There are not too many men who could pull off a sentence like that and all the women around us seem to take notice. I should feel… something. But instead, I let out a giggle.

“Okay Daddy, give me your hands,” I purr.

I take Cain’s hands and use them to cup my breasts. I press them together, leaning into him and crawling onto his lap. I straddle him, rocking up against him before I plant my lips on his.

He runs his hands down my back and settles them on my waist. When he parts his lips, I slip my tongue inside. I take my time, exploring every corner of his mouth. My fingers dig into his scalp.

When I pull away, I stare into his eyes. I give him my sexiest smile as I say, “Sorry Babe, nothing.”

“Not a damn thing.” He laughs and smacks my ass as I climb off of his lap. “What the hell is wrong with us?”

I let out an easy laugh, shaking my head. “I have no idea, but I don’t think either of us are getting any tonight.”

"Maybe not, but I sure as hell want to beat you over at the pool table. Get up, let's go."

I raise an eyebrow at him. "You've challenged the wrong drunk girl. You're on."

---

A half-hour into our game, Cain steps away to use the bathroom leaving his phone on the side of the pool table. When it vibrates, I can't help but look at the screen.

*Gabby: Are you going to stop by after your date?*

Now that's interesting. *Who are you Gabby and why would you both know that he's on a date and be asking him to stop by at this hour?*

When Cain reappears, he grabs his phone from the side of the pool table. "I thought I was going crazy, couldn't figure out where I left this." He opens it and I see a flicker in his eyes as he reads the message. "Hey, uh, I've got to run. I'll call for the Uber again…"

"Don't worry about it. I'm sober, I can wait. You should go." *Gabby, whoever you are, I've got your back, girl.*

"Are you sure?"

"Yeah. Have a good night Cain."

"You too." For the first time all night, light fills in the shadows under his eyes.

He hugs me and pays our tab in full. Cain may not be my person, but as a brother-in-law for my sisters, he's top-notch. Gabby has herself a good man right there. His exit is dramatic, a swift leap toward the open door, and just like that he disappears into the wooded area out front like a lumberjack Jacob-freaking-black.

All of a sudden, I feel a rush of inspiration. I pull out my phone and punch out the first draft of my new book. Axed out of Luck: A Whodunit in the Woods pours out of me as if it's being dictated by someone else. Every sense I have tingles and I know before it's even fully written that this is the book that is going to change everything.

# daddy vibes lumberjack

*Hideaway at the Lagoon Book Three*

# 30
# prologue: eloise

I can still hear the sound of kids yelling and parents cheering them on in the distance as I reach the start of the path. Trees soar overhead, their branches fanned out over my head in a canopy. You can't beat the view here, but I thought that parking my trailer in the woods would be more peaceful.

I crunch down the gravel road and with each footstep, I feel the pressure in my chest ease a little. I may have finally found the perfect location to write... at least for now. It's scenic, two of my three sisters are here, and it's peaceful.

But as my trailer comes into view, I hesitate. *The door to my trailer is open. Why is the door open?* That little tin can on wheels isn't just my trailer, it's my home, my writing headquarters, and my sanctuary. There's no way I would have left the door open, especially not with the deranged fans that have surfaced in the wake of my newfound success.

*Please don't be a deranged fan. Please don't be a fan.*

I take a deep breath and charge toward the trailer. If someone is there, I need to know. I don't need a damn lumberjack to come save the day. Whoever's in there is going to meet me and my can of pepper spray.

When I rip over the door, I'm stunned into silence. I have to blink twice at the sight before me just to make sure it's real. There's a kid. Well, not a kid exactly but a half man, half child person sitting at the small kitchen table. He's got a backpack sitting beside him and headphones pulled down around his neck.

*What in the world?*

He's holding my leather-bound writing notebooks and casually scratching into one of them with my new fountain pen. I can't think of a single more offensive thing. Those notebooks cost me a fortune. They were my gift to myself once I made it big and he's just... doodling. I slam my metal water bottle on the countertop behind him and he jumps with a start.

He looks up at me, eyes wide. "Sorry, I'll take off."

"Excuse you! What the hell are you doing in my trailer in the first place?"

The boy with the massive eyes looks up at me. He can't be more than fifteen, maybe sixteen. He's tall with lanky arms and a crooked smile. He doesn't look bothered by my outrage and when I pepper him with questions, he gives me a simple shrug.

"Well! What do you have to say? Those notebooks aren't for writing in." I press a hand to my temples in disbelief.

He gets to his feet but his eyebrows furrow in confusion. "But it's a notebook, this is exactly what notebooks are for." The ghost of a smile plays on his mouth as he holds up his sketch. Outrage aside, I have to admit that the art is pretty impressive.

"Okay, so you're not wrong." I cross my arms like some kind of crabby librarian and I don't even recognize myself right now. "But it's a special notebook for a story I haven't thought of yet. I've been saving those and now I... I'm not going to explain this to you. Why aren't you at lumberjack camp with every other boy in this town?"

"Ha. I've put my time in over the years. Believe it or not, lumberjacking isn't for everyone. I'm supposed to be a camp counselor this year, but I've been taking walks in the woods instead. Just, please, be cool about this." He holds his hands up and backs down the stairs. "Don't tell anyone. My dad's already got a lot happening right now and he's already worried that there's something wrong with me."

"I don't even know your dad." A wave of compassion washes over me and I start to wonder whether this kid is older than he looks or if he's just been through too much. "Stop it, there's obviously nothing wrong with you. Why would he be worried?"

"Oh I know I'm awesome." He lets out a chuckle as he steps out of my trailer. "He's the only one worried. It's because I don't want to be a lumberjack, I'm more of an artist type. It's a crime in this town."

I can't help but let out a laugh. "What kind of art?" I step outside behind him.

He turns back. "I don't know, I guess I've always wanted to be a writer or an illustrator." He shakes his head.

"You want to be a writer? I think you can do it, if you're committed." I watch his face and from the way his eyebrows raise I can tell I've piqued his interest. "That's actually what I do, I write thrillers."

He puts on his hat. "Cool. You could get some inspiration from the lumberjacks around here. Just a bunch of bros out chopping wood. Doesn't get much scarier if you ask me. You like writing dark stuff then out in this trailer? It doesn't get creepy?"

"Not until random kids show up inside of it." I let out a chuckle and he does too. "I never stay in one place for too long, so I don't worry too much about people finding me."

"I saw your fan mail. All that is fan mail, right? That's crazy." He gestures to the massive box on the table."

"Yeah, it is. I try to respond to it, but it got a bit out of hand after my last book."

"I'll answer them for you." He offers me a casual shrug. "Don't have anything else to do while I'm supposed to be babysitting the future lumberjacks of America."

"What? You want to answer my fan mail?"

"Yeah, it's not a big deal. You don't have to pay me. I'll come by tomorrow and grab a stack. Then I'll respond and leave them right here for you."

"Wait… really? I don't even know your name."

"I'm Justin. I'll stop by tomorrow."

As he walks away, a pang of emotion wells in my stomach. The kid is endearing, but there's something oddly familiar about him too. It could be the fact that my brother Nicholas wasn't too much older than him when we lost him. But Nicholas was never as soft as Justin.

I think the pang I feel runs deeper than that. I was pregnant once and it wasn't meant to be. But even before I knew how it would end, I could never picture myself as a mother. I couldn't imagine what my child would be like.

Somewhere in the back of my mind, I think that if my life had taken a different path, maybe my child would have been something like Justin. At least I hope he would have been funny, creative, and a little left-of-center.

I stare out at the gorgeous forest and inhale the crisp, clean, air. I've only been here a few days and Lumberjack Lagoon is already stirring up so much in me.

# 31
# eloise

"The phone calls won't stop. I'm literally waiting for the Red Dirt Motorcycle Club to open a Lumberjack Lagoon branch. They sure spend a lot of time worrying about what our family is up to for people who claim to hate us, I mean it's—"

"Go Tate! Come on!" My sister Nadia cuts me off with her aggressive cheering mid-sentence and I cover my ear. "That's my boy!"

"It's insane." I finish my sentence. And it *is* insane, even if Nadia doesn't want to talk about it.

When we lived back in Findlay, every single one of my siblings had some kind of entanglement with the local biker gang. It was a small town, and they were hard to avoid. But over the years, we've grown up and moved on, only the Red Dirt Motorcycle Club isn't ready to let us go.

Ariella, my oldest sister, had to literally disappear into the forest of Lumberjack Lagoon just to stop the stalking she was enduring from her ex and his groupies. They are power hungry control freaks and somehow they're reach extends all the way across the country. But at least they aren't here now… as far as I know.

The sun nearly blinds me as I look out into the lagoon. The kids out there are supposed to log rolling, but instead, they're just taking turns flailing around and falling into the water. I think I'm supposed to be making sympathetic noises like everyone else. Instead, I find myself biting back a laugh. Watching kids in Lumberjack Camp is entertaining, I'll give it that.

Still, as the sun beats down on me, I wrack my brain for an excuse to leave. This is the beauty of not having kids, you don't have to stay for the whole damn day. Nadia however is here for the long haul.

She's got a folding chair with a back on it, a visor, and a cooler with non-alcoholic beverages in it. When my three sisters and I found out that our deceased brother Nicholas had a son entering the foster care system, Nadia leapt at the chance to adopt him. I'm glad she did. She and her husband have taken to this parenting thing like fish to water… Or maybe more like lumberjacks to this lagoon.

*Buzz. Buzz.*

My phone vibrates in my pocket and when I check the number, a whip of discomfort washes over me. *Speak of the devil.* As much as I don't want to answer this call, I probably should. But I sure as hell can't do that right here.

I clear my throat. "Hey, I'm gonna head out."

Nadia turns to me in surprise. "Are you going over to the bookshop? It isn't open yet. Ariella isn't there yet. She and Caleb are just heading back into town."

I shrug, my phone vibrating with a voicemail. "I was planning on writing there today, so I'm heading over anyway. What's the benefit of your sister owning a bookshop if you can only go when it's open? I need to get at least three chapters over to my editor by the end of the week."

"I think it'll be all locked up," Nadia says.

"I'll take my chances."

I hop in my car and start my drive through the backroads of the forest over to the Hideaway at the Lagoon Bookshop. One of the many things that is starting to grow on me about Lumberjack Lagoon, other than the fact that the men are certainly something to write home about, is the fact that you can get anywhere in ten minutes. It almost feels like a place I could stay long term. Not now of course, but someday, when I get tired of wandering.

For now, I know that once people get settled around me, it's time for me to go. When I discovered that I wasn't ever going to be a mom, I decided that I needed to find the silver lining. No kids means no need to be settled. I get to move on when things get too real and have every new experience this life has to offer. That's a gift, especially for a writer.

I pull up outside of the bookshop. Writing in the back corner of Ariella's bookshop is inspiring. It's been kind of her to offer me a spot at the table by the window and the tiny back storage office to set up shop while I'm in town. With the glass front windows that overlook the forest, this place is pure peace… only, I can't get into the damn thing.

I walk from the front door to the back door jiggling every window latch along the way. Thanks to the ongoing threats from the Red Dirt Motorcycle Club and my new lumberjack brother-in-law Caleb, this place is locked down like Fort Knox.

"Dammit." I consider writing outside sitting on a tree stump under the canopy of branches. But I can't write thrillers and spend too much time alone in the woods. I get too sketched out and start seeing things that aren't there.

When I spot a window that's cracked open, I see my opportunity and act fast. It's on the backside of the building, and it's up high. But if I can get it open, it'd be enough space for me to slide through… I think.

It takes me a full ten minutes to roll a massive rock to the space beneath the window. It's heavy, and I don't exactly accomplish the task gracefully. I swear as I climb on top of a massive rock and pull the screen off in one tug. Feeling more confident than ever, I jam a stick in through the crack in the window.

"Ugh! Don't make me break you." I pound a fist into the glass just for good measure. "Come on you jackass!"

"No need for name calling." A man's voice bellows behind me and I turn with a start.

The flashing lights of a patrol car illuminate the man's massive frame. But he doesn't look like a cop. He's wearing flannel like he's cos-playing a lumberjack. With broad shoulders and rippling muscles, he definitely looks the part.

The man pulls all of my attention away from the task at hand and all of a sudden I don't care about getting words on paper. His piercing eyes stare into mine and I feel tingles whip down my spine. As he steps closer to me and my heart rate ticks up.

"What are you doing up there? Teaching that window a lesson?" He bites back a smile.

"Are you the sheriff?" I call down from the top of the rock.

"Yeah, that's how I got the car," he chuckles.

"But you dress like that?" I can't stop my eyes from raking up and down his body taking in every inch of chiseled perfection.

He tilts his chin up and a smug smile plays on his lips. "I'm the sheriff, but we're all lumberjacks here sweetheart."

# 32
# garrison

I can't stop myself from admiring the view of her full, curvy body standing above me, backlit by the sun. Her wild curls are pulled onto the top of her head in a loose bun. My stare lingers for a moment too long before I extend a hand to help her off the boulder. When she takes it, sparks ignite between us.

She tells me her story three times without changing a single detail. Now she's leaning casually on the hood of my patrol car tempting and teasing me with every response. In general, I don't do well with people who aren't transparent with me, but this woman is mesmerizing and she's driving me wild.

"Here's the problem I'm having. Last week these guys got a brick through their window. Apparently, some assholes half the country away are giving them trouble. Then I get a call reporting a break. We're here and you look a little guilty for someone who's supposed to be here. You tell me you live in a trailer with no permanent address. As far as I know, Ariella Greenwood owns this place and she's got one sister, Nadia. Can you see how this is a problem for me?" Ariella's husband Caleb and I have been friends for years, if he had another sister-in-law running around, especially one who looks like this, I think he would've mentioned it.

"Well officer, it looks like you need to keep up on the Lumberjack Lagoon gossip train. There are four of us sisters in total, Ariella, Nadia, and then the twins, me and Roslyn." She rolls her eyes at me and looks up from beneath long, dark, lashes.

"So you live in your trailer. But where is your trailer parked?"

Her mouth curls up at the corner. "Wherever I want to park it. Right now it's in the forest."

I furrow my brow in suspicion. "What do you do that allows you to roam around?"

"I'm not sure you're within the law interrogating me like this, but I write books if you must know, murder mysteries." Her words are a purr and I can't deny that it's sexy as hell.

I punch out a text to Caleb to verify the identity of this mystery woman. While I wait for his response, I continue my interrogation and she doesn't miss a beat. She somehow manages to turn my reasonable questions into something that sounds more like flirty banter. Far from looking nervous, Eloise looks turned on. Or maybe that's just me.

The sound of her phone vibrating pulls her attention. When she looks at the incoming call, something in her face changes. It's a flash of guilt that is unmistakable. For the first time, I know she's hiding something.

"You can take the call," I push her.

"I'm okay."

"Why? Who is it?" I can't help myself, there's something she doesn't want to share.

"What?" She swallows hard then snaps her head toward me. "That's none of your business." She clears the call and tucks her phone back into her pocket, her mask fully intact all over again.

For a moment we're at a stalemate. I can't decide if I want to arrest this woman or bend her over the front of my patrol car and teach her a lesson. From the way she's undressing me with her eyes, she seems like she'd like the latter. My mouth waters at the thought. We sit in silence while I decide if this woman is naughty or nice. I can't help but hope that she's on the right side of the law, though I don't know why I care either way.

When I finally get a response from Caleb confirming Eloise is his sister-in-law, I get to work helping her get inside. She follows me around the front of the bookshop and I pick up the fourth rock from the right, pulling the hidden key from inside of it.

"Are you freaking kidding me right now? There was a key the whole time. You could've just said that. I'm over here climbing on boulders."

I unlock the door and then hold it open for her with a dramatic wink. "It's all about who you know babe. I'm Garrison Staller." I hold out my hand to her when she takes it, another jolt of electricity runs up my arm and ignites a live wire within me.

"Eloise Astor, it's nice to meet you now that I know you aren't going to take me to jail. It's almost like you wanted me in handcuffs."

"You aren't going to jail, but keep talking like that and you could be in a lot of trouble."

I walk to the back of the bookshop and turn on the lights. I need to hit pause as everything in me screams to back away from Eloise before things get carried away. My life is already complicated. The last thing I need to do is involve another person in it.

It isn't just me I need to think about, I have my son to consider. Ever since my ex-wife decided that she was too big for this town, he's been a totally different kid. Not being reason enough for your mom to stick around is a heavy burden for a child to carry. I didn't cause the pain in my son's life, but I owe it to him to keep my focus trained on helping him overcome it. I blow out a deep, frustrated breath as Eloise unpacks her entire office on the wooden table in the back of the bookshop.

"Thank you for rescuing me today." She looks up at me with full lips and it's impossible not to imagine what that pretty mouth would look like wrapped around my cock. I might be a father, but I'm still a man.

"My pleasure. I'm going to leave you to it." It takes everything in me to turn and head for the door. But something in me can't resist turning back toward her to ask one more question. "How long are you in town?"

"I'm starting to think I'll be here awhile, but not forever. Somewhere in between those two. How long will you be here?"

"Forever." The word tastes sour as it leaves my lips. The reality is Eloise is probably another woman who is too big for this little town. At least this time I can stop the relationship before it gets started.

"Great! I hate to ask you for another favor, but I'm going to need your help again. I've written some police procedurals in this manuscript and I'm not sure they're very realistic. Any time you have to stop by and take a look, I'd appreciate it."

"I don't know." I shake my head.

"Come on, you can stop by while you're working. You know, serve and protect this bookshop and while you're here, maybe give me a few pointers."

I let out a chuckle. "I'll see what I can do."

# 33
# eloise

"It's in the culinary genre, there's got to be food involved." I bite back a giggle as Garrison's face curls into a playful scowl. "Not with the death in the story directly, but you know, maybe they are at a bakery or a new restaurant. Maybe they are dealing with cream puffs."

"You're kidding me. An entire sheriff's department stopped their day to look into a creme puff murder. That's unreal." He leans into me and heat bubbles in the place where our skin touches.

"Yes! Exactly, it's perfect. That's the genre. But taking some inspiration from my new temporary Lumberjack Lagoon residency, this new book is called *Axed out of Luck: A Whodunit in the Woods.* So in this case we're looking for a lumberjack-themed pastry."

"'Temporary huh? You are too big of a star for a place like this, I can see that." He raises a playful eyebrow at me.

"No, I'm a writer. I'm here for the big flash meet-cutes, but I'm not great at sticking around for real life."

Garrison grabs the stack of pink Post-It notes and a pen. "I'm a quick learner and I've got this whole writing thing figured out. He's the killer and he bakes her cookies. Only they aren't regular cookies, the chocolate chips are poison. The cookies are called Lumberjack Logs... Like normal cookies only bigger and more firm." He lines the sticky notes up with a wink and Garrison's dimples deepen as he flashes a charming smile.

"You're killing it, babe. If this whole lumberjack sheriff thing doesn't work out, then for sure you should be a writer."

Garrison makes me smile. It's only been a few days since we started meeting up at the bookshop, but I'm finding it hard to remember what life was like before he entered my orbit. The man talks to me like I've known him all my life. When he's not here, we're texting non-stop.

I've never felt so connected to someone who is basically a stranger before. He combs through the pages of my draft and I can't help but stare at him. With his chiseled jawline and brilliant smile, he's absolutely perfect.

I can't tell if the bookshop is unusually warm or if it's the hot current of energy sparking back and forth between us making me sweat. Writing with Garrison by my side is somehow better even though he has been terrible for my word count.

In the past, I've exclusively dated artist types, but seeing Garrison in his sheriff uniform does something to me. I feel myself inching toward him emotionally, but physically too. He feels the pull too, I can tell by the way he undresses me with his eyes, my exposed cleavage burning under his gaze.

"This is good, I like the cop as the romantic lead," he comments without looking up from the screen.

"I think I do too." The words slip out before I can stop them. I catch myself and add, "For now. I almost got tied down once and I'm not staying here for long. I'm an artist. We're always searching for more inspiration."

“You almost got locked down. What happened? You were married? A proposal?”

I swallow the lump in my throat. “No, a kid. Well, a pregnancy that didn’t work out.”

Garrison turns to face me. “Oh, I’m sorry to hear that.” He puts his large hand over mine and squeezes. Something about the sincerity of his thoughtful gesture almost pulls a tear from my eyes.

“It’s okay. My ex wasn’t exactly thrilled with the news to begin with, so when it didn’t happen, I think he was more relieved than anything…” I fade off but stop myself before I can run through the memories.

*Buzz. Buzz.*

“Oh, another voicemail… I didn’t even hear it ring.” I’ve been so wrapped up in Garrison everything else around me is slipping away.

I pick up my phone and listen to the message as Garrison continues to read. As the words crackle through my phone’s speaker,a slow-growing smile of disbelief stretches across my face. My heart thrums in my chest, hammering against my ribcage and my mind races. As soon as the message ends, I play it again. I can’t believe this is real.

“Wow,” I say when I finally hang up.

“Top secret writer business?”

“No, it’s not top secret at all. But it is kind of a big deal.” I bite back my smile. “They are optioning my series for Netflix streaming. It’s one of my wildest dreams to come true. You’re the first person to know.”

“You are kidding me! That is amazing.” Garrison doesn’t hold back. He grabs the leg of my chair and uses it to slide me beside him.

“Yeah, I wanted you to know.” As my books top the charts, my fame grows. Without meaning to, I've built a wall around myself.

But with Garrison, I want to share every part of myself. I want him to know me and the realization stuns me.

"Congratulations, Eloise,and thank you for sharing that with me."

The way he says my name makes the hairs on the back of my neck stand on end and goosebumps ripple across my arms. Then he wraps his arms around me and holds me in a hug that I never want to end.

Without giving it another thought, I lean into his embrace. In a moment of passion, I give in to the heat between us and ignite the spark with a kiss. Our lips connect and it sets my body on fire. I never want it to end. The world around us melts away and Garrison is all I can see. He explores my mouth and fireworks crackle between us. A current of heat runs through me as our tongues dance.

*Ding.*

The metal bell chimes against the door and it sends me leaping away from Garrison. He laughs and moves his hand inconspicuously to my lower back. Ariella and Nadia step in through the door mid-conversation. The last thing I need is my sister's input or speculation on my love life or lack thereof. My lips still tingle from the kiss as I try to play it cool.

"Hey, hey! How's the writing going?" Nadia sings songs across the bookshop.

"It's going. Garrison is helping me work through the police procedures." I don't know why I feel the need to explain his presence. Garrison has been here most days lately. Outside of that, he's best friends with my brother-in-law Caleb. Garrison doesn't need a reason to be at the bookshop.

*Ugh, keep it together before you give yourself away, Eloise.*

"Right, hi Garrison. We'll have both of the Staller's here in the next hour. Your sister should be here any minute." Ariella's tone is casual. If she saw the kiss, she isn't letting on. She turns to me.

"You've met Gabby, haven't you?" Garrison asks. "I assume that everyone in this town knows each other."

"Yeah, I think I met her here once when I first arrived. I just didn't know she was your sister."

Ariella continues, "Gabby's helping us come up with a plan for a welcome home party for Cai's return from his final deployment."

"I'm sure she's happy about that, Cain's got to be her favorite Greenwood brother. No offense to Caleb or Kai, of course." Garrison lets out a charming chuckle that I feel all the way to my core.

Before long Gabby shows up along with Ariella's husband Caleb, Nadia, and her husband Kai. It's a full on party and I'm ready for a good time.

# 34
# eloise

As the planning party for Cain's triumphant return gets underway, I give up on my hope of being productive. Beyonce on vinyl is blaring from the record player and there is a red and black buffalo-check box filled with pastries from Lumberjills Bakery open on the table.

I pull out a sugar cookie frosted in the shape of a man's beard and take a bite. The flaky layers dissolve in my mouth. I decide right then and there that writing simply isn't going to happen today.

Since I'm not going to get any work done, I focus all of my energy on acting casual and not giving away the burning desire I feel for Garrison. I'm desperate to talk to him. In fact, I'd like to magnet myself to his side after that kiss.

Instead, I keep myself away from him until a reasonable amount of time has passed. I eat more cookies, drink a cup of tea, and chat with my sisters all while secretly watching Garrison's every move. I notice a quiet confidence about him as he swaggers around the room that I can't get enough of.

I wait until he's standing with Gabby, then approach him in the most casual manner I can muster. As I walk up, I catch the tail end of their conversation.

Gabby continues, "...It could be easier if I pick him up today. He's been doing so much better he's been scribbling in that notebook nonstop, but I honestly think it's helping."

"Yeah, I think so too and that would be great." Garrison leans casually against a bookshelf.

"Hi, Gabby." I interrupt.

"Hey, Eloise, right?" Gabby's smile is just as genuine and brilliant as her brothers. *The genes in this family are unreal.*

"Yeah, it's nice to see you again."

When Garrison realizes I'm standing behind him, he turns with the start. His usual confident swagger briefly leaves him. I don't miss the flush of color that temporarily washes his face. It's probably just my imagination, but for a split second, I almost think he looks guilty.

I shake the thought away as soon as it arrives. As the three of us make small talk, I remind myself that not every man is a raging narcissist with something to hide.

"Gabby, let's get something on paper! Get over here lady." Ariella waves Gabby away from Garrison and me.

When she's gone, Garrison brushes my hand with his and his touch leaves goosebumps rippling up in its wake.

"I'd like to revisit that kiss." His words are a soft growl.

"Is that right?" I look up at him from beneath long, dark, lashes. "If you're serious, why don't you meet me in the back office in fifteen minutes." I raise a challenging eyebrow at him.

"I'll be there in ten." He lets out a chuckle and shakes his head. "I just can't figure out how someone like you is still on the market. You're unreal; beautiful, smart, sexy... Can't figure out how I got so lucky."

"Don't start that, you haven't gotten lucky yet. Would you look at that, only eight minutes left until my date with the handsome sheriff in the back office." I run my hand across his zipper as I walk away.

I watch the room as I pour myself another cup of tea. Everyone is wrapped up in their own conversations. There's a good chance if I slip out now, my absence will go unnoticed... So I do. I walk out of the bookshop's main room and into the tiny storage office in the back, closing the door behind me.

A few minutes pass and I watch the clock. At the ten minute mark on the dot, the door creaks open and Garrison steps inside. As soon as I see him, I'm overcome by desire and unable to resist the electric pull toward his embrace. I throw myself at him, wrapping my thighs around his waist and launching both of us backward onto a massive box of books.

# 35
# garrison

We lose our clothes in a frenzy of tugging and pulling until they are discarded carelessly in a pile on the floor. Eloise straddles my lap, her weight presses down on top of me. I wrap my arms around her warm, soft, curvy body and touch every inch of her supple skin. Heat radiates between us and the fire ignites. The anticipation of what's to come makes my cock throb with each heartbeat.

My lips run up and down her neck. I lick, kiss, and suckle at her until she lets out a breathy moan. Her tits in my face are impossible to resist and I slip a needy nipple into my mouth. Being this close to her I can feel as her heartbeat pounds in time with my movements.

She squirms on my lap as I reach between her legs and run my fingertips along her slick slit. Her folds are already drenched as I trace delicate circles around her entrance. When I slip a finger inside, she moans as she stretches around me.

Her hands clutch the packing slip on the top of the box, crumbling it into a ball of trash. Eloise's back arches with pleasure and she lets out a breathy gasp. I work on her until her moans fill the room and I know she's ready for me.

I pull my fingers out of her and put them to my lips. I'm hungry for her. My manhood pulsates and throbs with anticipation. Her musk smells heavy and even her scent makes me salivate. The heat in my core is so intense it burns, I'm desperate to be inside of her.

Eloise reaches between her legs and frees me from my boxers. I spring up to meet her, my tip already slippery. She strokes me and I feel her touch in every inch of my body. My body wracks with shivers and my pulse quickens. I melt with her touch.

There are so many sacrifices I've made as a single parent. Lack of sex has been one of the biggest for me. Now Eloise is on top of me and I'm aching with desire. If I'm not careful, she's going to send me over the edge with a simple touch.

She wraps her arms around my neck and she eases onto my dick. My hands settle on her hips and I guide her to the places I need her. I thrust inside of her and her walls hug me tightly, contracting around me.

The sensation is intoxicating. It's been too long and I'm too excited. I take a deep breath and force myself to hold on, savoring the moment. I keep her there for what feels like hours, slamming inside of her and making her mine.

The passion building between us comes to a head and her body racks with trembles. I bounce her on and off of me, claiming her. I give up on slow and steady. Instead, I throw my head back and take in every part of Eloise's beautiful body. Our passion is a flame that can't be quenched.

I strain, all my muscles tense as I drive her closer to the edge. Finally Eloise trembles and chants my name. The sound is irresistible. When she gives in to the tidal wave of pleasure, she takes me with her.

The release is earth shattering leaving me panting as I explode. Elosie collapses on top of me, her walls spasming around my firm length. I lift my hips to meet her, shooting hot streams of pleasure into her. She rocks forward, milking me to the last drop. Being with her makes me feel like a man. I'm overwhelmed with the desire to hold her close. She stays in my arms as the minutes tick by and we're washed in a blissful afterglow.

When she climbs off of me with a smile, I'm hit with a realization. Having Eloise once could never be enough. This magical night has done little to quench the insatiable hunger that gnaws at me.

I want more of her, all of her. I crave her touch, her laugh, her smile. I'm making up for lost time with a woman who has quickly become my whole world. Just like that, I'm addicted. When it comes to Eloise, I'm consumed by a burning desire.

Thankfully, it seems like Eloise feels the same way.

Our escapades don't end in the tiny storage room. I can't resist the pull toward her. It's impossible to bring her home, but over the next twenty-four hours we steal every minute we can together, ravishing each other in an endless cycle of passion and pleasure.

As much as I get lost in her, I know it's an impossible situation. I am well aware that I'm playing with fire by letting myself fall for her. She keeps reminding me that she isn't going to be in Lumberjack Lagoon for too long. She wants to keep things casual. This is a problem for me and not only because I'm falling in love.

I don't have the option to keep things casual. Eloise doesn't even know that my son exists. It isn't right to keep it from her. But if I tell her, I know we will be done before we get started. That is a reality I'm not ready to face.

# 36
# eloise

Two weeks pass and it's crazy how in love I am with Garrison, especially because, in reality, I hardly know the guy. Garrison has played his cards close to his chest from day one, but I have to. We haven't taken a true look into each other's lives. We haven't been able to keep our hand off of each other long enough to talk through the details of who we are or where we're headed. I haven't been to his house and he hasn't seen my trailer parked out in the forest. A part of me wonders if that's why this is working so much better than any relationship I've ever been in.

Still, lately, I do catch myself wondering about his life. I'd like to know what his place looks like. I wonder if he has any pets. I think about how he spends his time when he isn't climbing all over me, that is.

Garrison works a lot, so I've seen a lot of him in his uniform. He's been serving and protecting me all over town. We've made the nooks and crannies of Lumberjack Lagoon into our personal love nest.

You haven't lived until you've had a man in uniform bend you over the hood of his patrol car in the forest. He's found the time to take me on the stairwell of Lumberjills Bakery, in the empty cabins outside of Timber Logging, and we've done some questionable things beside the old fountain downtown. When it comes to Garrison, I can't get enough.

There's something sexy about having the relationship be our little secret. My sisters suspect something is up of course. But they have no way of knowing what's happening and I won't confirm or deny anything. If Roslyn was in town, that might be different. Hiding things from my twin has never been easy. But keeping Ariella and Nadia guessing is simple.

Having Garrison all to myself has allowed me to keep our relationship moving forward. But how much further can things progress if we keep each other at arm's length? I don't have anything to lose other than my unwillingness to stay here. But even that is making less sense by the day. Two of my sisters are here permanently, and my nephew is here, but more than that, I've started to day dream about a life with Garrison.

It's scary to let someone in again, but I keep reminding myself that Garrison isn't anything like any man I've ever known. He's honest and loyal to a fault. He and I have something that only comes around once in a lifetime, I'm sure of that. I've never felt more certain of anything.

Today, I'm back at the bookshop typing away on my next draft. While I'm writing, Ariella and Nadia are unpacking a new inventory of books and loading them onto shelves. This isn't exactly the peace and quiet I thought I needed to write. But I've grown quite fond of writing amongst the chaos.

Garrison stopped by this morning and he's been here ever since. He claims to be looking over my police procedural scenes. But in reality, he's taken to distracting me by tracing his fingertips along the outline of my thighs every time he gets the chance. The light touch makes heat bloom low in my stomach and I find it desperately hard to focus on anything else.

*Ring. Ring.*

As Garrison's hand runs up the inside of my leg under the table, I hardly notice the sound of the phone ringing behind the front desk of the bookshop. It's the shift in Ariella's tone that makes me take notice. Her face pinches into tight lines and her eyes go dark. It's enough to get me up from the table and over to her side. Nadia seems to catch it too. By the time Ariella hangs up the phone we're both standing by her side.

"Was it another empty threat?" I roll my eyes.

"It better not be," Garrison calls from the table. "I've had about enough of them."

"No." Ariella puts a hand on her stomach. "It's worse. That was the detective investigating Nicholas' death. It's been confirmed that the Red Dirt Motorcycle Club is responsible for the loss of our brother." She blinks back tears. "I suppose it isn't a shock at this point, but still. It doesn't bring him back but at least we have answers and our suspicions are confirmed. "

My head spins. Losing Nicholas at such a young age changed everything for our entire family. Now we know the men responsible for his death and they're the same ones who can't leave well enough alone.

A pit forms in my stomach. This is terrible news made more complicated by the one fact thing I can't share with my sisters. I'm tired of the phone calls and the secrets. But if I'm honest with them, they'd never forgive me.

# 37
# eloise

Nadia presses a hand to her temples. "We need to think about how and if we're going to tell Tate. His mom is still a part of that gang."

Ariella puts a hand on her arm. "You're his mom now. He'll be okay, he's got you, all of us, and a whole army of lumberjacks. But I am going to call Roslyn. She deserves to know too. Especially since she's still back in Findlay."

*Ding.*

The bell on the door captures my attention and Gabby steps in amid the chaos of the moment. When she does, the room is gravely quiet and she hesitates. "Uh, hi. Is everything okay here?"

"Gabby, everything is fine. They just got some news." Garrison hops to his feet and rushes toward his sister. He seems jumpy and caught off guard. He lowers his voice to a near whisper. "What are you doing here?"

I can't help but notice the odd change in his demeanor. It's out of character. But then again, everything feels different in light of what Ariella just shared.

"I came to drop off—" Gabby starts, holding out a backpack, but Garrison cuts her off.

"Right, yeah, I'll take that. Thanks." He puts a hand on her back and turns her around so she's facing the door.

I step toward them. "Garrison, why are you pushing her out of the door? It's okay. There isn't anything being said about Nicholas that she can't hear."

"She's just dropping off something, she doesn't have time to chat." There's an urgency in his tone as he puts his hand on the backpack.

I take a second look. The backpack is oddly familiar, though I can't place where I've seen.

Gabby pulls away from his grasp, jerking her body backward and taking the strap of the backpack with her. "Would you stop? What's wrong with you?"

"Gabby, we can talk about everything later." Garrison reaches for the unzipped backpack one more time and the contents explode out onto the floor.

From there it's a cascading river of school supplies. An iPad, pens, and a flurry of paper scatter across the floor. Garrison bends at the waist picking it up and shoving it back into his bag as quickly as he can. Amongst the items, I see something that makes my heart stop. It's a brown, leather-bound notebook with gold leaf edges. It looks expensive and I'd recognize it anywhere.

My eyes widen at the sight. "Uh…Where did you get that?"

"The backpack? It's—" Gabby starts, but Garrison cuts her off.

"It's mine," he says.

Gabby looks at her brother, eyes widening then pulling into a pinch. "It's whose?"

Garrison shoots her a pleading look that makes my heart race a mile a minute.

I clear my throat. "It's your backpack. If it's *your* backpack then where did you get your leather bound notebook? It's strange because that notebook is actually mine."

The whole situation starts to pull into a laser focus before Garrison says another word. I am trying to make sense of it all. But it's difficult when I feel every pair of eyes in the room heavy on us.

"You didn't tell her?" Gabby shakes her head. "I can't believe you actually didn't tell her. That is so wrong. Tell her the truth, Garrison. Do it now or I will." I don't miss the look of pure disgust that lands on Gabby's face.

Garrison on the other hand has fire in his eyes as he shoots daggers around the room. When he talks, his words are confident and bold. "Eloise, this is my son's notebook. His name is Justin. I didn't tell you because you keep insisting that this isn't serious and I didn't want to blow this thing up before it even started. But Gabby's right, he's my pride and joy. It was wrong of me not to tell you. Though, I do wish I could've talked to you about this in private."

My head spins with the news. Garrison has a child… A child I've been meeting with for weeks. A child who has poured out his soul to me about his father who just doesn't understand. It's a punch to the gut. I'm not meant to be a mother. I missed my chance. But anyone in a real relationship with this man will be a mother and that fact changes everything.

"I knew it! Ha! Fantastic. I knew there was something between the two of you, I told Nadia. Didn't I tell you, Nadia?" Ariella is the only one smiling and she quickly slaps a hand over her own mouth.

"This is a big secret." I cross my arms, my words snapping out in a rush.

"I should've told you. But I thought there was a chance you already knew from your sisters or Caleb. When I realized you didn't I don't know. I guess I wanted to keep you all to myself and not let the real world in."

"You lied." I cross my arms.

"Come on, that isn't fair. Don't act so innocent. Why don't you come clean too? Tell me about the person you've been slipping out to talk to all this time." There's no bite to his words, only hurt.

"Oh my god... who is the person?" Nadia's voice is a stage whisper behind me.

"No idea," Ariella says.

"Garrison stop, you don't know what you're talking about. I'll tell you everything, I just... Not here. I need time." I swallow the lump in my throat as the pressure mounts.

Garrison doesn't back down. "What are you... married?"

"What? No, of course not."

He continues, "Did you leave some poor, small-town sap who is still clinging to a scrap of hope with each phone call? This is just fun for you and that's why you don't want it to be anything serious, right?"

I put a hand to my forehead. When I look him in the eyes, I know for sure, he isn't going to stop. The time for truth is right now and once I drop this bomb, there isn't any going back. But he deserves to know, they all do.

"Stop it, Garrison. The person I've been talking to is a woman."

"Wow, I didn't see that coming," Ariella says. "Good for you! Love is love. I'm totally an Alli."

"Stop it, all of you." I turn and shoot my sisters a look, ny knees trembling beneath me. "I've been talking to a woman named Amber. She's Tate's bio mom and still heavily connected to the Red Dirt Motorcycle club. She's made some poor decisions, and she's fighting all sorts of demons. All she wants to know is whether or not Tate's okay, so she's been calling me. I know it isn't my place, but I've known Amber all my life and she's still a mom. She made the biggest sacrifice for her son and I thought she deserved to know that he's landed in the most capable hands."

Garrison's face softens. "I'm sorry. I shouldn't have—"

A sharp gasp sounds behind me and Garrison stops talking.

I turn to see Nadia, her mouth hanging open and a hand pressed to her chest. "Are you kidding me? How could you?"

"Dammit, Nadia I'm sorry." I start, but she walks away, disappearing into the backroom with Ariella by her side. I turn back to Garrison, fighting back tears. "Are you happy now?"

"That's how you blow up a room in less than five minutes. I can't believe you lied about being a father. That kid is the best thing that's ever happened to you." Gabby grumbles under her breath as she tugs Garrison toward the door.

When they disappear, I hear mumbles coming from a phone call to Roslyn in the back office. It's done. My sisters know I've betrayed them in the worst possible way and Garrison isn't the honest lumberjack I once thought he was. The room spins around me and I'm left feeling sick all alone in the empty bookshop.

# 38
# garrison

*Me: I'm picking you up early from Lumberjack Camp today.*

*Justin: No, it's cool, I'll stay and then walk home*

*Me: It isn't a suggestion, meet me outside in ten minutes*

*Justin: K*

I sit in my truck waiting for Justin to get in. Picking him up from Lumberjack Camp isn't something he's wanted me to do this summer, but today I'm happy I insisted. While I wait, I flip through the pages of scribble in the leather-bound notebook that ruined everything.

To my surprise, they aren't just doodles. The pages are brimming with poems, journal entries, drawings, and thoughts about being abandoned by his mom. There are things about me too, like how he thinks I'm too fragile to handle his big emotions. My heart shatters for my strong boy and the weight he's been carrying.

I read enough to feel more connected to Justin than I have been in years, but skip over the parts that seem too personal. When I close the notebook, tears flood my face. I'm both heartbroken at the silence he's suffered in and relieved to see that he has found an outlet, even if it's not me.

Justin's outpouring of emotion comes after years of begging him to talk to me, forcing him into therapy, and signing him up for every activity available in Lumberjack Lagoon. It's something to be celebrated. I'm just disappointed he didn't trust me enough to let me be a part of the process.

I have no idea how Justin ended up with Elosie's notebook, but writing in it has changed him for the better. It's just one more reason to love her.

My relationship with Eloise is irrevocably broken before it's even started. I've nearly ruined one of the best things that's ever happened to me. All I can think about now is salvaging it. My world opened up with love and laughter as soon as she stepped into it. She's shown me that happiness is still a possibility for me. I can't lose her now.

My chest heaves with the deep sadness of breaking the trust between us. I want Eloise in my life, not just now, but forever. I should've told her everything right up front. More than that, I should've trusted that her secrets didn't have anything to do with me. I've got to find a way to make things right before it's too late.

Justin pulls open the door of the truck and climbs inside. "Hey." His tone is calm and collected, but his eyes widen when he sees the notebook sitting on the seat. "Where'd you get this?"

"I was going to ask you the same thing." I start the truck. "You're clean for a guy who's spent his day out on a logging course in the woods."

"Yeah, about that..." Justin avoids eye contact and I watch the muscles in his jaw clench.

"You aren't in trouble. In fact, I think there are quite a few things I need to apologize to you for. I haven't been able to give you everything you need. That's on me. But I'm never going to stop trying."

Justin doesn't answer but he chews his bottom lip and nods.

"I'm gonna ask you to start by telling me what you've been spending your time doing. More importantly, where did you get this notebook?"

He lets out a long exhale. "I met a woman who is a famous writer. She's been paying me to answer her fan mail and it's given me a chance to write and draw. You know, I've been putting things on paper. I didn't want to tell you because I've been skipping out on lumberjack camp to pick up mail from her. She's been talking to me about why she writes and it's helped me get other things off my chest. Trying to figure things out the best I can..."

I don't take my eyes off the road, but something in me calms for the first time in a long time. "I don't care at all about Lumberjack Camp. In fact, this is the best thing I've heard in a very long time."

Justin sits up straighter. "She's the real deal, she even has fans who try to stalk her..."

From there, he explodes with animated stories about Eloise, writing, and what he's learned through interacting with her fans. I'm amazed at the passion that spills out of him and I sit hanging on his every word.

We pull up at home, but we don't make it out of the truck. Instead, it's my turn to come clean. When I tell Justin all that's happened between Eloise, he shakes his head at me with a chuckle.

"Dude, you didn't tell her about me? Like... who does that? Come on Dad, even I could've told you that was a bad idea."

"Don't I know it?" I can't help but laugh at Justin's reaction. "What I don't know is how you got so good with the ladies and how I'm going to fix this."

"I don't know either." Justin is grinning now. "But you've got to figure this out. Eloise is the best. Actually, I have something that I think might help…"

# 39
# eloise

"I need you to trust that I'm careful. I know what it feels like to want something so badly and then have it taken away. She's mixed up in some bad things, but when she called, I couldn't resist. In her moments of sobriety, she just wants to know that he's okay. And Tate is so much better than okay, he's thriving because of the life you and Kai are creating for him. I'm sorry I didn't tell you." My voice breaks at the end.

Nadia, Ariella, and even Roslyn sit side by side in the bookshop. They are a firing squad and I'm on trial. Nadia's shattered, betrayed face breaks my heart. I've pleaded my case from top to bottom. I've told them that Tate's mother knows Nadia and Kai are what's best for him. I told them that she wasn't a threat and that all she wants is an occasional update on the son she loves enough to let go.

"Eloise, I understand what you're doing, but I have to say it. This could easily become a safety issue. Red Dirt Motorcycle Club is still calling, making threats, and trying to find out everything about us and our new lives," Ariella says. "Just because some of them are in jail doesn't mean their reach stops. So you have to be careful."

"I know, I'm not stupid and I'd never put any of us at undue risk. Give me some credit." Thirty minutes into this cross-examination and there's no bite left in my words.

Roslyn lets out a huff and takes a sip from her tea cup. "It's true. I didn't want to say anything, but I've been followed home every night for two weeks. They haven't approached me or anything, it's like they're taunting me. Just letting me know they're watching."

I squeeze my eyes shut. "Why the hell didn't you tell us?"

Ariella shakes her head. "We could've at least sent Kai and Caleb to pick you up."

"I don't need some kind of lumberjack bodyguard." Roslyn folds her arms across her chest. "Although if I'm being honest, it was a little scary... That's why I'm not going back."

The bookshop falls silent and all eyes focus on Roslyn. My heart rate ticks up, this is almost too good to be true. *How did I not sense this? My twin telepathy has been so off recently.*

"What?" I blink at my twin in surprise.

Ariella clasps her hands under her chin. "That is the best news! We will make room for you here. You can stay at Caleb's old place until you get on your feet. You can be there for as long as you need. Until we figure out this mess with the motorcycle club..."

When their eyes wander back to me, I keep talking. I paint Tate's bio-mom in broad strokes until a picture of a selfless, brave woman who is struggling with hard things comes into full view. I talk until my sisters are nodding in agreement... at least two of them. It takes another thirty minutes of convincing before Nadia takes a sharp inhale. I wait with bated breath for her response.

"I don't think she deserves to lose all knowledge of her son. She's still a mother. That doesn't take anything away from me." Nadia speaks her words with a quiet resolve and Ariella wraps an arm around her shoulder. "It's going to take time."

I exhale. "Thank you for saying that. Nothing about this has to be fast. I'm on your side, you know I am." The knot over my chest loosens just a little.

"I do know," Nadia says.

She gets up and the tension in the room breaks just a little. Nadia flips on the electric kettle and I look at my sisters. They have to be the most incredible group of women I've ever known. I'm so grateful to have them in my life.

"Everything about Lumberjack Lagoon has drawn me in, but having you all close is such a good reason to stay put. Not that I needed one, Garrison is more than enough of a reason... If we can figure things out. And he comes with the amazing bonus of Justin. I just love—"

My sisters shoot curious looks at each other. Nadia shakes her head slightly and then turns away from me. I notice Roslyn bites back a smile.

My gaze bounces between them. "What are you not saying?" I cut my eyes at them.

"It's just that you messed that one up pretty good." Roslyn laughs and it pulls a giggle from everyone in the room. "We can all tell that you're officially in love and it's kind of fun to watch. The writer of death stories finds herself the star of a real-life romance. It's got a poetic justice that I just love to see."

"Stop it!" I laugh.

"I don't know what you're doing here wasting your time. You need to find Garrison and fix things," Nadia says.

"I know."

I pull out my phone and punch in a text.

*Me: Hey, I'm sorry. We need to talk.*

*Garrison: I was just about to call you. I'm sorry too. Come over and let's talk this through.*

*Me: Where do you want to meet?*

*Garrison: My house.*

# 40
# garrison

When she finally started speaking to me again, Gabby agreed to take Justin to the video game store and then back to her house for the day. Her only disclaimer was the un-shocking news that right now, she likes both Justin and Eloise so much more than she likes me. I told her that was not only fair but that I like all three of them more than myself right now too.

Before he left, I had the chance to talk to Justin about Eloise. As it turns out, their relationship has a longer history than ours. Tears spilled down my face when he shared the tremendous impact she's had on his life in such a short time. The kid already loves her just as much as I do. I can't believe I had the audacity to think that the changes in Justin were because of me.

The woman is meant to be in our lives. I've never been more sure of anything. Eloise rounds out our little family perfectly. I've got to make sure she knows that. Today is my last-ditch, Hail Mary-style attempt at winning her back for good. It won't be big or flashy, I know she wouldn't want that. But I'm putting all my cards on the table... I hope it's enough.

When Eloise arrives, I meet her on the porch and wrap her in a tight hug. She doesn't pull away from me and I take that as a good sign. I keep her there tucked close to my chest. The thought of this woman not being a part of my life makes me sick. I memorize every one of her details. I take in the floral scent of her hair and the feel of her curves pressed against my hard line. I can't handle the thought of losing her.

Pulling away I take her hands in mine while I get the words out. "I'm sorry, Eloise. I didn't tell you about Justin because I was scared to ruin things between us. I'm sorry I haven't been honest about the fact that you have quickly become my favorite person. I've been promising to keep things casual while falling head over heels in love with you at the same time. I thought it'd scare you the way it does me. But I'm not afraid to tell you that I love you. I don't want you to move on and there isn't anything casual about this."

She squeezes her eyes shut and tears spill down her cheeks. "I love you, Garrison. You are the reason nothing else has worked out and I'd go through it all again to end up here with you."

"Give me the chance and I'm going to make things right starting now." Taking her by the hand, I pull her in through the front door. "This is my home. There's the kitchen, the living room, and on this side of the house is my bedroom."

Her eyes roam the family photos on the walls as she wanders down the hall. "I like it here, it's very… you. I can't believe the view you have, it's incredible. What's down the hall?"

"That's where we're headed." I take a deep breath as we approach Justin's bedroom door. "My son Justin is sixteen years old. He's the light of my life and I'm proud of the person he's become. What you can't possibly know is how closed off he's been since his mom left. Sulking, quiet, and impossible to reach… Until now. Now he meets up with an incredible, inspired writer who encourages him to be himself. It's made all the difference in the world."

She smiles. “He has got to be the coolest kid I’ve ever met. Getting to know him is healing parts of me that have been broken for a long time.”

My chest swells with pride at the thought of the two most important people in my life forging an unbreakable bond. “You can’t imagine how happy that makes me. I have something for you, I’m sharing this with you with Justin’s permission. When I asked him if he had anything to say to you, handed me this. He said you’d want to see it.” I grab Justin’s iPad, open his drawing app, and hand the device to Eloise.

For a moment she just stares. Then her mouth falls open and her eyes widen. Then she flips through the pages and a smile pulls at the corners of her mouth.

“He is so incredibly talented.” She dabs at the tears that fall from her eyes. “This is my book. He’s turned it into a graphic novel. Justin is amazing, he could do this for a living if he decides to. I’m so honored that he’d share this with me. Thank you for showing me this.”

“You should know that he’s only been creating art and writing since he met you, but it’s worked wonders for him already. You’ve healed something in him without even knowing it. That goes for me too. I’m a better man since you’ve come into my life and I’m ready to share every part of myself with you if you’ll have me.”

Eloise’s eyes glisten with tears as I take her into my arms. “I’m ready for this, for all of it.”

I plant a kiss on her lips. Our tongues dance until heat rushes across my body. We seal the promises both spoken and unspoken between us. There isn’t any going back now. Eloise is mine forever.

# 41
# epilogue: eloise

It's been twelve full weeks. When I first discovered I was pregnant, I couldn't fend off the sense of unease. It's like I was immediately transported back in time. I relived the blocked memories of my first pregnancy… telling my boyfriend, seeing the panic flash in his eyes and the cold hard chill of betrayal when he abandoned me. It was the worst time of my life and I didn't want to go down that road again.

I decided to give myself time to grow into the realization that I'm going to be a mother before I share it with anyone, including Garrison. He and I are still together and stronger than ever. I've parked my trailer on the land behind his house. Only now, it's more of an office.

My place is in the bed beside Garrison and just down the hall from Justin. We didn't make a big ordeal of moving in together. It happened naturally. It was the two of them asking me to stay one night at a time and me deciding that there wasn't any place I'd rather be.

Life is sweet with Garrison in it and I can't imagine ever

wanting it any other way. We haven't talked about marriage because we haven't needed to. I know that I will love him my whole life. Of course, a baby could complicate things.

As my pregnancy has progressed, most of my fears have been replaced with a sense of calm. I feel connected to this tiny person growing inside of me. I know without a doubt that I will do anything to keep him, or more likely her, safe. It's just a guess, but my intuition is heightened.

Being pregnant hasn't changed me into a new person. As I look down at my growing belly, there's no denying that it fits in a way I could've never predicted. I still don't think I'll go about parenting in the same way as Nadia, but I know I'll figure it out. I'm like a new version of the same old me, just more stable and ready to love on this little girl.

Today I'm telling Garrison. There are so many things to consider. First off he's already got an amazing kid that he's almost done raising. He told me that there was a time when he envisioned himself at the center of a large family, but that was when Justin was little. Starting over could be daunting after all he's been through.

It hurts to consider, but I've already promised myself that I won't ask Garrison to stick around if he doesn't want to be involved. I won't ask him for anything. It would hurt, but it's a possibility I need to make my peace with. I've had twelve weeks to watch my stomach swell and my body change. I know this is right for me and I hope it's right for him too.

*Creak.*

When the door opens, Garrison steps inside and my heart leaps into my throat. Justin is with Gabby so I have to act fast.

"There she is," Garrison bites back a massive grin that sends tingles whipping across me.

"I have to tell you something." The words blurt out of me and my heart thuds against my ribcage.

He chuckles. "Okay, I hope it has to do with me peeling that top off of you." He wraps his arms around me from behind and plants a kiss on my neck.

I turn to face him, taking his hands in mine. "No, Garrison, I'm serious. I need to tell you something… I'm pregnant."

As soon as the words escape my lips they hang heavy in the silent space between us. Garrison stares, blinking, his face unreadable. All of the fears I've been casting off and holding at arm's length come crashing in around me as he puts his face in his hands.

The truth is I don't want this to be easy on him. I want this even if it's messy or hard. More than that, I want to tackle this life with Garrison by my side. Another truth billows up inside of me… I have no control over how he might react.

There's a very real chance I might be in the same situation all over again. The thought sours my stomach. I take a sharp inhale of breath to hold back the floodgate of tears threatening to spill down my cheeks. The sound seems to jolt Garrison back to the present.

A slow-growing smile stretches across his face. "You're pregnant. This is," he blinked back tears. "This is incredible." His words are soft, but I hear every one of them.

One simple sentence undoes a lifetime of damage that Garrison never caused in the first place.

Garrison grabs my forearms and pulls me in tight to his chest. "Thank you, I can't wait to do this with you. What a gift."

All of my anxiety washes away. He stands in front of me, solid as a rock and stable enough to hold me, Justin, and our new baby together for a lifetime. For the first time in my life, I let myself get excited about the possibility of being happily ever after. Garrison puts a hand low on my stomach. Tears well in his eyes and it all feels too good to be true.

"Sweetheart, you are already an incredible mom. You might not have been there in the beginning, but there is no doubt that you are changing the trajectory of his life. Now... this. I can't believe how lucky I am. I can't wait to see you with this little guy."

"Thank you, I'm so happy. You are my favorite person and I can't imagine doing this with anyone else. This baby is going to have the best dad." I look up at him through blurry, teary eyes. "Also, you should know that it's a girl... probably."

A soft laugh escapes his lips. "Well if I'm going to have a tiny Eloise on my hands, I'm in trouble."

# protected by the lumberjack

*Hideaway at the Lagoon Book Four*

# 42
# prologue

***SPECIAL ALERT: Breaking News for residents in the Findlay Farms community and surrounding areas. Dangerous suspect at large. The Findlay Farms Sherriff's office has issued the following warning to all residents as the manhunt continues.***

*Just seventy-two hours ago, a female victim, Roslyn Astor, was taken with force from her bedroom after an intruder gained access through an unlocked side door of her townhouse. The woman managed to escape after kicking out the truck's back window while at the gas station and spraying the assailant with gasoline. Eyewitnesses say she stood over the fuel-covered man holding a lighter above her head. She threatened to ignite a flame multiple times before police detained the suspect and the perpetrator was taken into custody.*

*After further investigation, police have deemed the suspect, Leon Raven, to be infatuated with the plot of Taken Twins, the best-selling novel written by the victim's real-life twin sister, Eloise Astor.*

*The suspect was released after twenty-four hours on a half-million dollar bail bond. The suspect failed to show up for a mandatory court appearance this morning. Officers are unable to locate him at his home or place of employment. They did find letters and photos indicating a history of stalking and have since elevated his threat level to the community.*

*Members of the public are advised to be on the lookout for a tall man with a thin build and curly blond hair. He was last seen wearing a green t-shirt that says, Read Banned Books. Any persons with information as to the whereabouts of Mr. Raven are encouraged to contact the Findlay Farms County Sheriff's Office as soon as possible.*

# 43
# roslyn

"Get up."

The voice booming over me as I lie in bed sends chills down my spine and I gasp for air. I must be having a nightmare after what happened a few days ago. My eyes snap open and I find that my bedroom is still dark.

But then a flashlight illuminates. It isn't crazy bright, but it's the middle of the night and it doesn't take much to blind me. This is most definitely not just a nightmare. My heart rate ticks up and my breath catches in my throat. My world hasn't made sense in a long time, but this is wild, even for me.

*It's the middle of the night, so why the fuck is there someone in my room? I can't go through this again.*

"Roslyn, get up."

I squint at the recognition in the tone. "Eloise? Eloise, what the hell are you doing here?" I bolt upright and glare at her. "You drove across the country and came to my home in the middle of the night and snuck in like some sort of creep, to what? To freak me out?"

Eloise puts a hand on her hip and flips on my light. "No, I didn't come to freak you out. In fact, I called, texted, emailed, and called the groomer only to find you haven't worked there in weeks. Then I see a news article that so kindly informs me that my sister has been abducted by one of my readers. So yeah, I'm here in the middle of the night."

"Well, you wasted your time because I'm fine. He isn't going to come back here." Even as the words leave my mouth, I wonder whether or not I believe them.

"Based on what? Based on the good faith of a man acting out the plot of my murder novel? Unreal. Your window isn't even fixed. You're getting in the car and we are taking you out of town until he is behind bars."

"Oh my god, you're literally insane. I'm not going anywhere and what do you mean *we*?"

"Ariella and Nadia are in the car with all of your belongings."

My eyes widen as I take in my room. I haven't lived here long, but what little possessions I did have are in fact gone. Fire spreads through my chest. This is just like my sisters. The three of them rallying together and making decisions about my life is right on par with what I've come to expect from them.

I've become an expert at disappearing, even in this little town. I change jobs, houses, and friends. I'm a ghost on social media. Yet here my sisters are the single entity that I can't keep away from me.

"Give me an hour." I get to my feet and stomp my way into the shower. When the water hits me I'm invigorated with a second round of complaints and I shout them loud enough for Eloise to hear me. "If I'm so helpless, how come I'm not dead right now? Huh? Did I sit back and let that stalker who you turned loose on me through your stupid book take me? No, I didn't. I fought back. I almost lit him on fucking fire. Maybe you should go find him. Kidnap him, he's the one who needs protecting..." My rant goes unanswered and eventually, I run out of steam.

When I step out of the bathroom, I find the final scraps of my life have been tucked neatly into the back of a massive white pickup. The only question left is who's lumberjack-husband loaned it to them for the journey since all three of my sisters have married men with big axes. Kai, Caleb, and Garrison are real-life Paul Bunyons.

I get in the car in silence, slamming the door like a toddler to put a little more emphasis on how I feel about being abducted for the second time this week. Nadia backs the truck out of my driveway in silence. No one dares to say a single word until we pull onto the highway.

Ariella, my oldest sister, turns to look at me from the front passenger seat. "We tried to contact you in a million ways. We were worried about you and the sheriff's department recommended that we get you out of town until this lunatic is behind bars."

"Yeah, Eloise told me."

"It's not a joke Roslyn. This guy has a record of some disgusting things. He had only been out on probation for a short while. Did you know that?"

My blood runs cold. "No, I didn't." I don't think I've let myself fully process the traumatic events of the week.

"We heard from your old coworkers that you'd opened a dog-walking business. Do you know how easy it would be for someone to do something terrible to you while you're out all alone in a park?" Ariella's eyes go glassy. "I can't even think about it."

I bite the inside of my cheek. "I'm sorry I didn't get in contact with anyone. I'll stay put until this thing passes."

The car goes quiet again and I can feel the collective exhale of tension leaving the cab when I lean back against my seat. I would ask where we're going, but I think I already know. All three of my sisters have moved to a tiny town in the Pacific Northwest called

Lumberjack Lagoon and they are completely obsessed. Even Eloise, *traitor.*

The longer we drive, the more my anger fades. Instead of anger, my body racks with the fear I've squashed back over the last week. My sisters do me the solid of ignoring the tear that slips down my cheek as we put miles between me and a man who is obsessed with having me dead.

We move from silence to catching up. We start with trash TV and the books we've been reading. But then, they move to real life and I'm reminded of the whole life my sisters have built without me. They are chasing down dreams they didn't even know they had and I'm happy for them. I'm grateful for my sisters. They are all I have in this world. As much as I hate to admit it, a part of me needed a full-blown rescue mission to help me get out of my own way.

While they chat, I reflect on my own life and find there aren't many loose ends to tie up. But I do need to call my dogsitting clients because it seems like I'll be unavailable for a few days. I pull out my backpack and search the pockets.

"I need my phone. I thought I grabbed it."

The car falls silent.

"Where is my phone? Did I leave it?" I don't miss the looks being passed between my sisters and I already know I'm not going to like whatever they're about to tell me.

Eloise lets out a heavy sigh. "You didn't leave it. The sheriff's department advised you to go completely off-grid until Leon Raven is back in custody. He's been pretty sophisticated in his hacking skills and they're worried that he will find you."

My mouth falls open. "Unreal. All this and now no phone too because some small town sheriff said so."

"It isn't just the sheriff's office. We were worried sick and we want to follow all the advice we are given," Ariella adds.

"Alright, I get it."

I fold my arms across my chest and close my eyes as we make our way to the middle of nowhere. Falling asleep isn't difficult since I haven't gotten much of it for the last few days. By the time I open my eyes again, the landscape is unrecognizable. What was once long stretches of open sky is now a green treelined forest.

We pull off the highway and the road winds in a never-ending pattern of switchbacks and gravel roads. I can't imagine anyone living way out here, let alone a stalker following me all this way. A surprising sense of peace settles around me.

The car comes to a stop in front of my sister's adorable bookshop, Hideaway at the Lagoon. A woman with curly dark hair and a gregarious smile meets us in the car. Ariella opens her door.

"Hi, I'm Gabby. I'm so glad you made it."

"I'm Roslyn."

Gabby is Eloise's new sister-in-law and I like her immediately. She makes her way to the bed of the truck and unloads my suitcase. I breathe in a sharp inhale of fresh, crisp, mountain air. I've been out here once before for a wedding and I have to say, there are worse places to be stuck.

Gabby, Ariella, and Nadia make their way inside the bookshop. I sling my backpack over my shoulder and follow suit.

"Uh, hold on a minute." Eloise puts a hand on my shoulder. "You aren't staying here."

"What are you talking about? Stop it already, I'm exhausted."

"Staying with one of the three people you know in this world isn't exactly hiding... We've got somewhere else in mind for you." The ghost of a smile plays on the corner of Eloise's mouth as another massive truck crunches up the gravel path beside us. "Kai and Caleb's cousin is going to keep you safe for a few days in an undisclosed location."

"No, that's where I draw the line. I'm not doing it." I grab my backpack and push the car door open. "There's no way."

When the truck door swings open, a man with broad shoulders and a chiseled jawline underneath a beard steps out. His white t-shirt clings to every one of the muscles in his chest. His arms are covered in tattoos and his eyes are dark and pooling.

My body responds to him in a way I'm not prepared for. A long simmering ache that's been pushed aside bubbles up to the surface. I make a decision right then and there. I can either spend my time running from this man or being naked underneath him. Right now, I'm liking the sound of the latter.

He stops my thoughts in their tracks as he puts his hand out to mine. "I'm Beckett Oakes, I hear my job is to keep you safe for the next few days. You can trust me not to leave your side."

I put my hand in his and try to ignore the way sparks shoot through me. "I'm Roslyn, it's nice to meet you."

*You can trust me not to leave your bed.*

# 44
# beckett

It's been twenty-four hours of being alone in my cabin with Roslyn Astor and it isn't what I thought it'd be. When Caleb first told me his sister-in-law was being stalked, I figured I'd do him a favor in keeping her safe for a few days. He promised me a few paid days off of work to get the job done and it seemed like a good deal. I had no idea that being with Roslyn like this would be so intoxicating.

She is a spitfire of a woman. I imagine whoever abducted her was immediately filled with regret when she fired right back at him with gasoline. She didn't want to talk about it at first, but I pulled the story out of her.

Roslyn is a fighter and I love that about her. On top of everything else, she's stunning. With her curvy body, dark eyes, and sunkissed skin it's easy to see how someone could get obsessed with her. But that doesn't mean it's been easy to contain her here.

Today, I've found myself hiding out in the treeline on the path right behind my cabin because Roslyn thinks she's sneaky. She doesn't make a sound as she steps off my back porch and looks over her shoulder at the back door.

I tuck myself out of sight a way down the path and watch the sun dance off her curves with each step she takes. It's impossible not to imagine what it'd be like to have those long legs wrapped around me. But when she steps off the path and into the dense forest, I know it's time for me to stop fantasizing and catch up.

Roslyn may think she can disappear, but I know these woods like the back of my hand. I cut a path in the opposite direction and loop around the tree. I wind up at a boulder that she will have no choice but to pass. She doesn't realize that the Oakes family compound is massive but gated. When she heads up the path, a self-satisfied smile playing on her lips, I clear my throat.

Roslyn jumps out of her skin and she whips her head toward mine. "What the hell?"

I let out a chuckle. "You know what, I can see why you got kidnapped. You're terrible at this. I saw you getting ready to leave from a mile away."

Her head snaps toward me. "Dammit Beckett. Don't you have a tree to cut down? What are you doing following me?"

"I'm being paid to follow you, sweetheart, and enjoying it too if I'm being honest."

She rolls her eyes and bites back a playful smile. "Well, I don't need you to follow me every second. I wasn't trying to escape, I wouldn't put my sisters through that. I'm just getting some fresh air. I thought I saw a dog back here. I think it could've been a bear or a cougar too. But I wanted to find out—"

"Find out and then what? What the hell is the plan after you slip away from me with your kidnapper on the loose and a possible bear?"

She folds her arms across her chest and I watch her cleavage swell, rising and falling with each breath. "Making plans that work out in my favor isn't exactly my thing these days. Nothing makes sense right now, so I guess I just figured I'd see what happens."

"Well then, I'll figure it out with you." I hold out my elbow to her.

Roslyn hesitates for a moment before slipping her arm through mine. The feel of her skin touching mine sends a shock wave of heat rippling through me and I shake the sensation out of my fingertips. There's something about being here with Roslyn that feels surprisingly right. She's the breath of fresh air I didn't know I needed and I can't get enough.

When we get back to the house, I ask Roslyn what she wants for lunch, and she tells me she normally has a protein shake… She says it with a straight face and I'm appalled. I shake my head in disgust and pour her a second glass of wine while I fire up steaks on the grill.

She sits across from me in a black tank top and too-big sweatpants looking like the sexiest woman in the world. I find that I like taking care of Roslyn. With the alcohol in her, she's more chatty than she has been and I want to hear every word of what she has to say.

"...My plan wasn't really a plan. My ex was older than me and he kind of set me on this path to be the perfect wife. You know, marry rich and live in a big city. His path became my path. Now I'm here in a lumberjack town of all places." She lets out an adorable giggle.

"Hell yeah, you are." I flex my bicep and wink at her as I bring our plates over to the table. "I'm sorry you aren't living your big city dream. But I don't think there's a dude in that city who can cook up a steak like I'm about to serve you. Give this place a chance."

"Yeah, I'm starting to think I probably should. That might just be the wine talking though." She bites her lower lip and, drink or no drink, the look she's giving me isn't something you can fake.

"Let me ask you a serious question. What did you want to do before this creep groomed you to be his trophy wife?"

“I wanted to be a vet.” Her smile fades and a flash of emotion washes her face.

“Why’d you change your mind?”

“He uh, my ex, he made it difficult to continue. He made it difficult for me to trust anything. Hell, he made everything difficult. I don’t want to talk about this. It’s ruining a perfectly good night if you ask me.”

I take her hand from across the table. “Okay, you don’t have to say anything you aren’t comfortable with.” I drop the topic, but I can’t forget the look of hurt on her face. A fierce wave of protectiveness washes over me. “Are you good? Do you want more food, water, or another glass of wine?”

“I’m good, except…” She tilts her head to the side and the corner of her mouth pulls into a smile. “I do wish we had fucked already.”

# 45
# roslyn

Things move in a frenzy from there. One minute, he's pushing me back against the wall and devouring my neck. The next I'm tackling him onto the couch. He goes down easy for being a bear of a man.

From there, I straddle him and he springs to attention. He's rock-hard with desire beneath his jeans. I roll my hips and rock forward, giving him a show he won't forget. I feel his hands roam every inch of me until he peels my shirt off over my head and reduces it to a crumpled pile on the floor.

"If I had known that this was in the job description, I'd have been a whole lot faster to say yes." Beckett's words come out through gasps of breathy moans until I slap a hand over his mouth.

He sucks my fingertips until I move them and dig into his scalp. Then Beckett peppers my mounds with kisses. He circles my needy nipple with his tongue, slipping it into his mouth and creating an electrical current that zaps between us. I feel him pulsate beneath me.

My back arches with pleasure as fiery tingles of heat whip through my body. I let myself get lost in the warmth of his mouth on my skin. Beckett knows how to touch me and it drives me wild with anticipation. My insides ache with the desire to be filled by him and I grind onto his lap desperate for more friction.

"I need to be inside of you." His words are a growl as he wraps his fingers around my throat and pushes me onto my back.

He peels off my clothing and his pants are quick to follow. Then Beckett works his way down my body. He drops off the couch and onto his knees in front of me. When he puts his hands on my inner thighs, I let my legs fall open for him.

Beckett plants hungry kisses on my glistening slit. When he finds me already drenched, he parts my lips with his tongue. Each rotation of his tongue has me jumping in time with his movement. My heart rate beats in a frenzy of lust. With his face buried between my thighs, he laps at my folds.

He works on me until heat builds low within me. I thrust my hips up to meet him. Beckett's name slips off my lips like a prayer as I chant it into the ceiling of his cabin and beg him not to stop.

By the time he's lining himself up with my opening, my insides are desperate to be filled. Beckett shoves inside of me in a single thrust. His wide head is burrowing deep within. My tight walls wrap around his girth and the friction sends shock waves of pleasure through me.

When he rocks into me, his movements are in perfect rhythm with mine. Our bodies connect in white-hot bliss until Beckett is all I can see. We stay there for what feels like hours rhythmically pulsating in time with my movements.

A wave of pleasure builds low within me as the heat between us reaches a boiling point. His breath comes quickly, matching mine as he picks up the pace. Beckett's hands roam every part of me, tangle in my hair, and move back down to my thigh.

Tremors shoot through me and I bear down on him as my body quivers. When he thrusts one final time, my walls have no choice but to collapse along his length. I let go with a small scream of ecstasy ripping from my lips. Beckett keeps pounding until he's falling over the edge with me and I ride him until the last drop.

We lay there panting in the blissful aftermath of what can only be described as the best sex of my life. Beckett wraps me in his arms and every part of me melts. He has me two more times before the sun comes up. Every moment with him is more incredible than the last. He has captivated me in a way I could've never imagined and I never want to leave this cabin.

---

Our one-time wild night becomes a favorite pastime. Beckett and I start a cycle of making love, talking until the early hours of the morning, and drifting off to sleep in each other's arms. I find myself wishing that this pretend life we've created together was real.

Now the sun is coming up on my third day of blissful captivity and Beckett is tracing the outline of my curves with his fingertips.

I look back to find his eyes wide open. "You can't sleep? What are you thinking about?"

"It isn't that I can't it's that I don't want to. I don't know how long I'm going to have you here and I can't imagine it ending. Playing house with you is too good and I don't want it to end. After this, I'm afraid I'll end up some sort of Facebook friend and that could never be enough."

"Let's not think about that right now." I slide my hand beneath the sheets and run my fingers across his chest. "Besides, I don't even have Facebook."

"Why don't you have any social media?"

"My ex made a revenge porn video of me without my knowledge. He posted it all over the internet. It's the very first thing that comes up when you search for my name. I worked with a legal team for a while and got him to take it down. But that's the thing about the internet, nothing ever goes away. Since I couldn't get rid of it, I got rid of myself. I quit applying to schools and pulled down all my social media. It's stopped me from a million things I wanted to do." Saying it out loud eases the weight of the burden I've carried in silence for so long.

In response, Beckett only pulls closer to me. "That son of a bitch better hope I never meet him. I'm sorry that happened to you, Roslyn. You've had shit for luck when it comes to men and I want to be the man who changes that."

His words make a lump well in my throat because I think he already has. Beckett drapes his body over mine, holding me tight until I drift off into a peaceful sleep.

# 46
# beckett

Every time I think we are done with our sex bender, Roslyn drops to her knees and wraps that pretty little mouth around my dick. We spend the next days naked and locked in this push and pull of passion. I take Roslyn up against the wall, on the kitchen counter, and outside in the clearing behind my cabin. Her curves make my mouth water and I can't get enough.

Now the sun is peeking in through the curtains in my bedroom. But it's the sound of my phone vibrating on my bedside table that has me peeling my eyes open. Roslyn is still sleeping soundly and looking like an absolute angel.

I slide my arm out from under her and roll onto my side to get turn off the damn buzzing. I clear the call from my cousin Caleb. Whatever it is can wait. Nothing is as important as what's about to happen in my bed. I trace the outline of her breast with my fingertip. Roslyn's skin is smooth and warm to the touch.

*Buzz. Buzz.*

Just when I'm adjusting my pillow and disappearing into a world where only she and I exist, my phone vibrates again. This time it's a text message. I roll away from Roslyn and check it. But when I do, I have to read the message twice.

*Caleb: Ariella is wondering when she's going to see her sister again.*

*Caleb: Roslyn did get her phone back, correct?*

*Caleb: What's going on? Why haven't you brought her back yet?*

My mind races. I guess I put the reality of the situation out of my mind a few days ago. The truth is, I like having her here. But I can't keep Roslyn locked up forever. If I ignore Caleb, he's sure to come out here. It's amazing he hasn't shown. But as soon as she knows Leon Raven is no longer a threat, I'll never see her again. She's made it clear that she won't stay here and she doesn't strike me as the type to keep in touch. I can't have that. I can't lose her. I—

"What are you doing?" Roslyn's voice isn't sleepy, there's an edge to it that has me jumping to attention.

I snap my phone shut. "Nothing, I'm not doing anything. Good morning, beautiful." I lean in to kiss her, but Roslyn pulls away from me.

Her face pinches into tight lines and she raises an eyebrow. "Why do you look so guilty if you weren't doing anything? Really, tell me, what were you doing on your phone?"

I shake my head. "I wasn't doing anything. I was waiting for you to wake up and—"

She sits up. "Oh my god, were you taking pictures of me? Beckett, please tell me you weren't taking pictures of me. I can't go through this again..." Roslyn pulls the blankets around herself, covering her naked body.

"You don't need to cover up, I just had those in my mouth, remember?" I let out a chuckle but she doesn't so much as crack a smile. I lean back against the headboard and a knot tightens over my chest. "Would you stop it? Of course not, I don't ever want another person seeing you. I want to keep you all for myself. I was checking a text message." I let out a long exhale. "They uh, they caught the man stalking you."

"No way! That's great news. That guy is a fucking creep and now I don't have to worry about him and neither do any other women." Roslyn's face pulls into a smile and her eyes widen. "Wait, why aren't you excited? I'm sure you don't want that guy running around any more than I do. When did they catch him?"

"Um," I run a hand over the taut muscles in the back of my neck. There's no use lying now. It will only take a single Google search to find out. "They caught him a few days ago."

She tilts her head and her eyes rake over my face. "Oh? And you just found out?" Her words are clipped at the end and it makes a lump form in my throat.

"No, dammit, I didn't. It's been a few days. I was going to tell you. I just never found the right time to bring it up. Okay? I'm sorry. Is that what you want to hear?"

Every muscle in her body goes rigid and she's out of bed in an instant, reaching for clothing.

"Don't, come on I—" I start, but she isn't listening.

"Give me my phone. I want to leave, now." Roslyn folds her arms across her chest. "You saved me from a stalker by keeping me prisoner. What a hero." Her sarcasm stings and my stomach hollows out.

"You don't have to leave, I'll drive you where you want to go."

"My phone Beckett, now. I'm going to be making my own decisions starting right this minute."

"Okay, I'll get it." I slip my boxers on and retrieve her phone from the locked glovebox of my truck.

By the time I'm back inside she's fully dressed. When I hand it to her, she powers it up immediately and steps outside to make a call. It only takes her sister ten minutes to crunch up the gravel road that leads to my cabin. Another two minutes and she's out of my life forever. As I watch the car disappear, my stomach swirls and aches.

Roslyn is the most incredible woman I've ever met. She makes me feel like the man I want to be. Having her here all to myself has been a dream and I know what I did was wrong, but I wouldn't change it. She and I are meant to be, now I just have to figure out how to make her see that.

# 47
# roslyn

Nadia picked me up with my nephew in the car. It was a perfect excuse to drive back to town without having to offer a single word of explanation. She dropped me off at the Hideaway Bookshop with no questions asked. Three hours later, I lean across the counter, staring at the clock. Time is moving in slow motion, I'm sure of it. This place is empty today and Eloise has taken to writing her books at one of the back tables.

Ariella is unpacking a shipment and grinning at me from ear to ear. "Aren't you happy it's over? He's in jail for good this time and you are free."

"Yeah, I suppose it's good that no one is trying to stalk me, abduct me, or kill me at the moment if that's what you mean. At least not until my darling twin over there writes another book some psycho wants to act out." I try for a smile, but the muscles in my face don't want to cooperate. It's like my body knows that Beckett isn't here. "Here, Ariella, Let me do that box for you."

She hands it over and I make my way toward the psychological thrillers, I feel Ariella's and Eloise's eyes on me, tracking my every movement. They aren't going to let this go without an explanation and so I beat them to the punch. I tell them all that's happened with Beckett and how I left.

On cue, Eloise chimes in. "Let me get this straight. The dude lied to you and made you think that the stalker was still out to get you. Is that right?" Eloise shakes her head.

"Pretty much, yeah. It's wild behavior, right? Who does that?" I mutter, but my words have no bite, only sadness.

Eloise lets out a strangled laugh. "There are two types of men who do that. The one who is bat shit crazy in general and the one who is so crazy about you that he doesn't want to lose you. So which one is Beckett?"

"Hmm, probably the second kind." I let out a laugh.

"And you are equally crazy about him then?" Ariella's voice perks up at the end in an annoying little sing-song.

"Stop, what do you want me to say? Yeah, of course I am. The truth is I feel lost without Beckett in my world. I know that sounds crazy because we've only just met, but every part of my life makes more sense with him in it," I snap.

"Awwwwwww." My sisters mock me in unison.

"What are you going to do about it? He's out there somewhere feeling just as devastated as you are," Ariella says.

The thought makes my chest ache. "I might have overreacted a bit and had Nadia pick me up."

"Who, you? Overreact? Never, I don't believe it." Eloise smirks at me.

"I'm going to make my way back over there and at least talk to him."

*Ding.*

The bell on the door to the bookshop chimes and it has my head turning on a swivel. Beckett steps inside and I jump to my feet. I'm thrilled he's here and there's no way I'm having this conversation in front of my sisters.

I meet him close to the front door and when he wraps an arm around me, I melt into his embrace. "Come on, let's talk outside."

Beckett's eyes sweep the bookshop and he seems to understand the situation immediately because he stops on a dime. In one movement he laces his fingers with mine and pulls us toward the door. We keep walking until we are out by his truck and away from prying eyes.

Beckett lets out a soft exhale. "I'm sorry, Roslyn. I should have told you immediately and handed your phone back to you. I didn't because I wanted to keep you all to myself. Meeting you is the best thing that's ever happened to me and I was desperate for it not to end.."

"You should have told me because I don't want this to end either. You are my favorite person and the only thing that makes sense in my crazy world." Beckett wraps his arms around my waist.

He lifts me effortlessly off the ground into a hug that has my heart rate ticking up and butterflies flapping in my stomach. Beckett holds me there for what feels like a lifetime and the whole forest seems to disappear around us.

"I got you something." He opens the passenger side door of his car and pulls a shiny laptop off the front seat.

I tilt my head in confusion. "Wait, you got a computer… for me? Beckett, that's sweet but you know I hate the internet."

"Stop it, just trust me on this one. Open it and try searching yourself." His eyes pool and sparkle in the sunlight.

Tension rises in my throat. "No, this is cruel—"

"Trust me." He puts his hand on mine and I realize, I do trust him.

My fingers tremble as I open the lid and tap my name into the search bar. Old, familiar feelings of disgust whip through me. But all of that subsides when the search comes up empty. I try again, opening a different browser and clicking on my name… Nothing. Adrenaline courses through me and my my mouth falls open. This is too good to be true. The videos are gone.

"How?" I can hardly speak through the tears welling behind my eyes. "How did you? Is it just this computer or something? They can't really be gone, can they?"

"They are gone from every computer. I had Gabby wipe your records from the internet. You've got a clean slate. Now you can do anything you want to do without having to hide out. I will always keep you safe. So if you want to walk dogs forever, do it. No one is going to touch you. If you want to go to vet school, you can do that too. I'm happy as long as I'm the man by your side cheering you on."

I look up at him through teary eyes. Beckett understands me like no one else. My whole world is better with him in it and for the first time in a long time, I don't want to leave. I want to stay exactly where I am, right by his side.

# 48
# epilogue: roslyn

I hold the letter in my hands and it feels too good to be true. My eyes run across the words over and over again... *Roslyn Astor, we are pleased to welcome you to the online University of Veterinary and Animal Science.*

All of my dreams are coming true and I have Beckett to thank. He has come into my chaotic, scattered world, and made it all make sense. Not too long ago, I could hardly imagine a stable life in one place full of opportunities and lumberjacks. Now I can't imagine my world any other way.

Beckett loves me exactly as I am. He is a shield between me and anything standing in my way. My heart thuds in my chest as I think about sharing the news of my acceptance into the program with him.

I park my car outside of Ariella's bookshop. My shoes crunch on the gravel path beneath my feet and I can't help but walk quickly toward the door. I'm not expecting to see the whole gang gathered together when I step inside, but it's for the best. I know my sisters and Gabby will be thrilled to hear the news. But I want to make sure I tell Beckett first, he deserves that.

"Hey, is Beckett here by chance?" My voice sounds more casual than I feel.

"No, we are planning the launch party for my next book. As it turns out, we'll be just in time for my brother-in-law Cain to come home from his final deployment. Gabby and I are thinking of combining forces and having a big blowout bash. But something tells me that party planning isn't really Beckett's scene." Eloise lets out a laugh.

"That's strange, he told me to meet him here." I pull out my phone to double-check the message.

Beckett says he's on his way and I wish he'd hurry. This news is burning a hole in my pocket. I haven't had anything to be proud of in so long and this is a total game-changer.

"You're hiding something." Eloise drums her fingers across the table top and raises an eyebrow at me.

*Stupid twin-intuition.*

"I'm not." I tuck a strand of hair behind my ear. "You two must be getting excited for the triumphant return of the final Greenwood brother." Caleb and Kai have two brothers, Kameron who passed away, and Cain, the baby in the family. Bringing Cain home from his final tour with the military is at the top of my mind for this group and I can't blame them.

"Sure I am, as much as anyone else is, I mean." Gabby's face flushes in a way I don't expect at the mention of Cain's name. As far as I know, she was in a serious relationship with Kameron before he passed away. So why is the thought of seeing Cain making her blush? She tucks a strand of hair behind her ear and turns away from me.

*Crunch.*

The sound of a car on the gravel outside has me forgetting all about Gabby and rushing for the front door. I get outside before Beckett can even get out of his truck. He looks as sexy as ever when he greets me with a kiss that makes my heart flutter.

I throw my arms around his neck. "I have something exciting to show you."

His mouth pulls sideways into an irresistible smile. "And I have something exciting to show you."

"What, you do? Okay, you go first then." I hold my acceptance letter behind my back.

"Okay, but I'm warning you, this is going to be hard to top." Beckett reaches into his pocket.

"I don't know, mine is pretty good," I let out a giggle as he takes my hand. "Where are we going?"

"Away from prying eyes." He winks at me and tingles whip up and down my arm.

We walk up the path until the bookshop disappears from sight. When we get to a clearing lined with wildflowers, Beckett stops walking. He reaches behind a massive boulder and pulls out a bouquet of flowers.

"I've thought of a million ways to do this, but I know you so well, and I knew having an audience wouldn't be your thing. I knew I was in love when being trapped in a cabin with you felt like the biggest blessing I've ever experienced." His eyes well with tears. "I love you so much. I want to be the man by your side through every fresh start. I want to be the constant because now that I know a life with you, there's no way my life can be the same without you."

My jaw falls open and I gasp when he pulls out a tiny black box. *Yes. Yes. This is right. I want to be with Beckett forever.* My heart feels like it might burst out of my chest. When he snaps open the box, a sparkling ring glitters up at me. The gold band is topped with a brilliant diamond but the truth is I don't need a ring at all. Just loving

Beckett would be enough. My breath catches in my throat and my eyes well with tears.

Tears stream down his cheeks. "Roslyn Astor, you are the love of my life. I want to protect you, keep you safe, and make sure you get wherever it is you want to go. I love you with all my heart. Will you marry me?"

"I will, you've made me the happiest person in the world. I love you so much."

Beckett gets to his feet and when he stands, he lifts me off the ground. In this moment, everything makes sense.

# captivated by the lumberjack

*Hideaway at the Lagoon Book Five*

# 49
# gabby

*Bark. Bark.*

I'm expecting company, but the sound of a dog is new. I look out through the front window of my cabin and smile when Buck bounds out of the big, white truck. His fluffy tail swings from side to side with his every movement and his happy tongue dangles from his oversized mouth.

It's been two years since I've seen Kameron's dog running toward my front door. It catches me off guard and a rush of nostalgia floods me. For a split second, I lose myself in time and my heart rate ticks up. But I shake my head and reality comes back to me just as quickly.

In the past two years, I've learned to live with grief hitting me in the strangest ways. But this reminder in particular feels extra cruel. Footsteps crunch on the gravel walkway towards me as I fight to stay in control of the swirl of emotions floating through me. I swallow the lump of sadness, and guilt in my throat and try to ignore the joy. I ground myself with the cold hard truth. But my breath comes in short, hot gasps.

*My fiance Kameron isn't here anymore. We could have been married by now. Buck should have been our dog. But Kameron never made it out of that truck. Life is moving on. I am happy without him and that is okay.*

A rush of tears floods my eyes in spite of my best efforts. My vision blurs as a knot ties itself over my chest just in time for Cain to turn the handle and push open my front door.

"Hi." Cain's charming grin pulls an instant smile from me, even in the midst of my emotional chaos.

"Hi, I'm happy you're here." Buck bounds over to me and I bury my face in his soft fur. "Hi buddy, I'm happy you're here too. It's been too long."

"Hey, save some for me." There's humor in his tone, but Cain's grin fades as he takes in my expression.

I swipe at my tears, trying to keep them at bay as I get to my feet. "Last night before the big send-off." My smile quivers at the corners.

Cain wraps his arms around me, pulling me tightly into his broad chest. The warmth of his body surrounds me in a comforting and protective shield. The steady beat of his heart thuds against my cheek as he holds me close and keeps the rest of the world at bay. I relax into him.

When he lets go, he holds me out only far enough to look me in the eyes. "What is it? What's the matter?" Cain strokes his thumb across my jawline.

"Nothing." I bite back my emotions and let out a stabilizing exhale. It's a skill I've mastered in the last two years. "I didn't expect to see Buck is all, it caught me off guard."

Since Kameron passed away, his dog Buck has become the shared property of his three brothers, Caleb, Kai, and now, apparently, Cain too. The four Greenwood brothers were thick as thieves, so it makes sense. They are the only people in the world who loved

Kameron as much as I did. I can understand why they would each want to spend time with the only living piece of Kameron left on this earth.

Cain hesitates for a moment, then nods in understanding as he walks past me into the kitchen. His white t-shirt clings to his broad shoulders and falls across his chiseled chest. He pulls a bowl from the kitchen cabinet. He fills it with water for Buck then opens the refrigerator, grabs two beers, and puts them on the kitchen table.

He pulls out a chair and gestures for me to sit beside him. Cain's quiet self-assuredness puts me at ease. My breath comes back to a natural rhythm as I slide into my seat.

Cain puts a hand on the leg of the chair and pulls my chair toward his. "You don't have to give me a perfect answer. But I want to know what's going on with you. I'm here with you and I love you even when it's messy." His hand grasps at my thighs sending a wave of heat whipping through me.

Cain's quiet compassion is all it takes to break the floodgate. We've had hundreds of talks like this in the last two years and Cain understands so much without my having to say it. "It's all of it. Buck bounding toward me. Me being in love with Kameron's little brother. We've been living in a bubble with you constantly being out of the country on deployment. But do you know how weird our situation sounds when you stop and think about it?"

Buck paws at the door at the sound of his name and Cain lets him out back. "I don't think about how it sounds to anyone else because I know what I want. I don't give a shit what it sounds like to be honest with you." He shrugs and his forehead wrinkles in confusion.

"I know you don't, but you have so many people who love you no matter what, even when you aren't perfect. My parents wouldn't understand and..." A rush of heat floods my face and I bite my bottom lip. "And then there's the fact that you're leaving again."

Cain sits again, this time turning our chairs to face each other. He puts his hands on my shoulders. "For my final deployment. *Final.* I'm coming back here to you in a few months and then we can finally be a normal couple." His words are slow and steady. "Then I get to spend every day waking up with you in my arms. I want that life so badly I can taste it."

"I do too, it's just scary. What you're doing is dangerous. What if you don't get to come back? I can't lose another love in my life." The thought strangles the words as they leave my lips and I can't hold back the tears as they stream down my cheeks.

"Hey, I need you to trust me. I'm coming back. I'm not going to leave you." Cain turns to face me, he clutches my face between his palms. "I love you Gabby, I'm never going to leave. That isn't how things end between us."

Cain's hands move from my face to my hair. He keeps me there until my breath syncs with his. He holds me in such an intense gaze that goosebumps ripple across my arms. He doesn't say anything, but the truth screams back at me. I'm captivated by this man who treats me like I'm the most important thing he's ever held.

Cain saw me at my worst and chose to stand beside me. He's never broken my heart, but he has sure as hell taken on the task of mending it. I close my eyes and when I open them, Cain moves in closer to me.

The pull towards him is irresistible. I close the distance between us without giving it another thought. My mouth lands on his and fiery heat crackles between us as our tongues dance. The kiss takes my breath away.

# 50
# cain

My heart races as her feather-light touch glides across my skin. Zaps of electric heat tingle as they whip through me. This isn't the first time we've given in to our desire to be together. My body aches in anticipation of what's coming.

In the beginning, Gabby claimed that these moments of passion between us were isolated incidents. She felt guilty and I admit that I had my reservations too. But this fire smoldering between us is undeniable. If there are any hesitations left, they are drowning in our hunger for each other.

By the time my lips are peppering her neck with kisses, she's acting on instinct. Her fingers dig into my scalp and I pant as I wrap my mouth around her nipple through her thin shirt. When she slides off her chair and drops to her knees in front me, my heart rate ticks up.

Her hands tremble as she unzips the front of my jeans. My eyes darken as I watch. My manhood pulsates in anticipation of her touch. Gabby is the only woman I've ever wanted every part of. She's it for me mind, body, and soul.

Even with my size, Gabby takes me into her mouth. I feel my tip hit the back of her throat, but it doesn't slow her down. Her tongue runs along my length before he sucks me into her hollowed cheek.

I wrap my hands in a fist full of her hair as every muscle I have contracts. A fluttering sensation rises in my chest. She has this way of being vulnerable and sexy as hell all at the same time. This is all I've dreamt about every night of my deployment. Every inch of me is ready for her, but I don't want to explode yet.

There's something about the way she keeps looking up at me from beneath long dark lashes as she bobs on my tip that has me right on the edge. Gabby keeps sucking until I have to pull out of her mouth in a frenzy. The fire in me is ignited and there isn't any going back.

Panting, I stand and pull her to her feet. When I tug her into the living room, she comes willingly. We hardly have time to reach the couch before I push her onto her back. I peel Gabby's clothes off and mine are quick to follow.

I take a minute to memorize every inch of her gorgeous, curvy body. It's all I'm going to have to get me through the long nights in the coming weeks. But I can't think about that now. I'm focused on the way her body comes alive with my touch. I trace her curves. When I get between her thighs, I find her folds are already slippery for me.

My manhood throbs and pulsates with a desperate desire to be buried deep inside of her. Caging her in with my arms, I line myself up with Gabby's slick opening. When I push inside I can hardly breathe as she collapses around me. The friction has me twitching with desire.

Her walls expand and flex around me until we fit like a glove. It's like she was made for me. From there all it takes is a single powerful thrust for our two bodies to become one. I rock inside of her with a rhythmic motion that drowns out everything around us.

Gabby wraps her arms around my ribcage and surrenders to me. Clinging to my chest and moaning my name into the ceiling. The heat building between her soft, round edges and my hard lines makes it impossible to keep ahold of myself.

I keep her there, rocking into her, losing myself in the woman who makes me the man I want to be. Waves of pleasure pulsate through me as I claim her over and over again. When Gabby's muscles clench and release around me in time with my movements I know she's close. I pick up the pace as intensity builds low inside of me.

"Cain."

The sound of my name on her lips makes my breath hitch as I pound into her, driving her closer to the edge. When she lets go, tremors rack her body. Every muscle she has tenses as she rides a wave of ecstasy.

She arches her hips and my release is quick to follow. I let go, shooting hot streams into her. Gabby takes in all of me, clenching, and milking me to the last drop.

But we don't stop there. I take her two more times as the sun sets in the forest over the top of the treeline. Hours pass like minutes before we finally collapse in each other's arms. Even then, I don't let her go. I hold her tight to my chest as her eyelids grow heavy and I kiss her forehead when she falls asleep.

I know she worries about our future and what people will think, but I've made my peace with the situation. My brother was one of the best men I've ever known. His time on earth was too short and there isn't a day that goes by where I don't miss him.

He made a huge impact even by being around only a short time. That includes keeping Gabby's heart safe. Gabby thought that he was meant to be her forever. We all did. Even now, as much as it would hurt, I'd give her up if I knew Kameron was back, waiting with open arms.

But the harsh reality is that he isn't coming back for reasons I'll never understand. We are all here left to pick up the pieces. Kameron didn't want that for any of us. He wants us whole and happy. That's why I think my brother played a hand in bringing Gabby and me together. He knew we were going to need each other.

The love Gabby and I share has grown from the darkest of times. There isn't anything I wouldn't do for her. Once I get through this final deployment, I'm going to spend the rest of my life proving it to her.

# 51
# cain

*Gabby,*

*I know it's only been a few weeks, but I can't stand the thought of making it eight more without seeing you. Right now, I can picture you sitting in your stock tank pool underneath the branches of the evergreen behind your house.*

*If I were a betting man, I'd guess you're hair is pulled up into a bun on top of your head. You've probably got some kind of crochet project, half dangling from your arms. The bottom of it is wet from being dipped in the water while you are busy watching birds, squirrels, or TikTok videos. I know you don't care much for them, but I love your quirky imperfections. Ugh, I'd give anything to get tangled up in that yarn with you right now.*

*It's crazy how you've become my whole world in the blink of an eye. I'm desperate to touch your skin and tangle my fingers in your hair. I close my eyes and see your perfectly round tits in my face and your naked body all over mine.*

*You changed me. Apparently, I'm now the kind of dude who writes love letters from a makeshift tent a whole world away. But I'm embracing it. I don't want to go back to the life I knew before you.*

*The truth is, I lost a part of me when I lost my brother. I was scared to retire from my military career because I didn't think anything was waiting for me in civilian life. There's a reason most people don't stop working until they're old. When you leave your job, you lose your purpose. But now that I have you, I've got my purpose. I know that I'm meant to spend the rest of my life loving you and I'm going to do one hell of a good job.*

*This isn't new to you, but I thought you might be needing a reminder at this point. It isn't a proposal either, at least not an official one. But that's not because I don't want to marry you. I want to marry you more than anything in this world. But when I make those commitments to you, I want to look you in the eyes so that you know I mean every word.*

*For now, I have a surprise for you to help pass the time. While I was home, I took to brushing Buck while I had him. I noticed an incredible amount of fur falling from him. Well, I asked around and one of the ladies down at the bookshop helped me find a place to spin his fur into yarn for you.*

*I know Buck is over with Caleb right now, but I thought having a part of him with you might be a comfort while I'm gone. If you look in the drawer of the nightstand on my side of the bed, you'll find it.*

*I'll see you in just a few weeks my love and dream of you until then.*

*Cain*

# 52
# gabby

*Dammit. Go on you stupid thing.*

I'm supposed to be deep into my IT work at home today. But how can I when the day I've been waiting for is finally here? So instead of being at my kitchen table, I've got my computer open at a back table in the Hideaway Book Shop. I'm not typically *a bump the mouse so you look active* kind of employee, but I can't help it. I'm on edge and it's impossible to focus.

I tug at the black yarn Cain thoughtfully had spun for me from Buck's hair. It was such a sweet gesture. Immediately upon finding it, it's been my dream to make a tiny crocheted version of Buck using his own fur. But right now the project has turned into a beady-eyed demon dog that is more creepy than cute.

"Hey." My sister-in-law Eloise sits down at the table across from me and I toss my creation onto the wooden chair beside me.

"It's nice of you and Ariella to let me work from here the past few days."

"Anytime." She leans forward to stand, but then hesitates. "But especially today, right? With the big party and all." She smiles.

My eyes flick to my computer screen for the first time in an hour. "Oh that's right, Cain Greenwood is making his triumphant return home today, isn't he?" I aim for casual, but I don't know if I hit the mark or not. It's hard to be casual about an event you've been counting down to for weeks.

"How are you feeling lately?" Eloise leans back in her chair.

I squint at her. "Great. How are you feeling?"

She lets out a breath. "Yeah... You know, your brother and I were talking and... well, if there's anything you want to tell us, we are here for you. All the way. No matter what."

My blood runs cold. "What do you mean? Don't be crazy." I let out a half-hearted laugh. My hand flies instinctively to my belly but I jerk it away as soon as I think better of it. "I feel completely fine. I was just about to get up and help Garrison with the balloons right now." I stand and march toward my brother and the helium tank. "Only in Lumberjack Lagoon can you find buffalo check balloons. That's the crazy thing. These are going to be the perfect touch."

*What the actual fuck did Garrison and Eloise figure out? Do they know about Cain? They can't. There's no way he'd tell anyone. If that isn't the case, do they know about... my... condition?* I blow out a deep breath and squash back every emotion I'm not ready to tackle.

Eloise is close behind me as I reach the front of the bookshop. My eyes fly to the clock. Cain could walk through that door any minute and I need to keep it together.

"Garrison, Gabby is feeling just fine. Isn't that a relief? I'm going to leave you two to chat. But it can't be overstated how far in your corner I am. Just, you know, in general." Eloise gives me a smile and squeezes my shoulder as she turns to walk away.

When I look up at my brother, it makes me want to turn and beg Eloise to stay. A part of me is desperate to throw my arms around my new sister-in-law like a child and beg her to stay while I tell my brother the secret I've been avoiding saying aloud, even to myself.

I close my eyes and swallow back my guilt. When I open them again, Garrison is wearing his empathetic face. It makes my lips quiver. "I'm thirty-three and an adult and this isn't the time or the place. This is a celebration and a coming home party… This isn't about me. So whatever it is you think you know can wait for another time. Now pass me a balloon." My heart thuds in my chest.

Garrison folds his arms across his chest. "You're pregnant. I didn't believe it at first, but after Eloise pointed it out, it is all I can see. Are you okay?"

His words suck all the air out of the room as reality washes over me. Garrison is right of course, but I'm not ready to think about it and I'm mad as hell that he's forcing it on me. My mind swirls with a thousand things to say. But I don't trust myself not to cry.

I open my mouth to let it all out, but only two words come. "I am."

"Okay, you're going to be okay. I'm going to help you. But you have to start by telling me who the father is, I'm not going to freak out on him. Well I might, but in the end—"

"Stop it. I can't." I look around at the room filled with all Cain's friends and family. My stomach lurches. "I'm not ready to talk about this."

Garrison lowers his voice. "We need a plan in place. You aren't going to do this alone no matter what. I'm going to be here… we all are. But this guy, whoever he is, he's going to meet his obligations. I'm not going to stand back and let some dude—"

"Stop it. Seriously, what year is this? You aren't going to fight anyone for my honor. It isn't like that anyway. I'm going to figure things out in my own time. All I need from you right now is to shut up." My legs tremble underneath me.

"Look at the banner!" Ariella Astor, Elosie's sister and the owner of this bookshop bounces between Garrison and me. "Sorry, I've got to step on this table to get this thing up. It says, Army Pack to Lumberjack. So clever, right? What a perfect title. Did Eloise tell you I helped her come up with it? She might be the big-name author, but when it comes to throwing a themed party for a brother-in-law, I'm sure she couldn't do it without me..." Ariella trails off and looks back and forth between us. She tucks a strand of hair behind her ear. "Sorry, am I interrupting?"

"Not at all. Your timing is perfect. Here, let me climb up there and give you a hand." I pull the stepstool toward the table.

"Like hell you are." Garrison puts a large hand on my shoulder and pushes me away. "I've got it."

I shoot daggers into the back of his head as Garrison climbs onto the table. Once he's got both hands over his head and Ariella's task list, I take the opportunity to walk the other way.

The tables are stacked with tiered trays of sugar cookies provided by Lumberjills Bakery. There are drink stands and jars of wildflowers lining the walkways. It's a gorgeous bookshop and even though it's big, the place has standing room only. The room is alive and buzzing with energy. Cain has so many people who care about him and for good reasons.

I force a smile and try to fit in. After all, as happy as they all are, I can't imagine anyone is more excited to see him. My heart is so torn because the minute Cain walks through that door, everything is real. I don't know how he'll react. It isn't fair to tell him the minute he arrives. But keeping it from him feels wrong too.

Then there's the elephant in the room. I don't know how the rest of our family and friends are going to take the news that the girl who was once Kameron's fiance is now pregnant with Cain's baby. The room feels warm and I clutch the edge of a table to steady myself.

*Ding.*

The metal bell on the door to the bookshop chimes and just like that my time is up. Cain steps inside flanked by his brothers Caleb and Kai. People make their way toward him, but I'm frozen in place. All of a sudden it's hard to breathe. The room moves in slow motion and my head starts to spin.

"Gabby, Gabby." The sound of my name brings me back. "Are you okay?" Eloise looks up at me, her face twists into tight lines of concern.

"What's the matter?" Garrison's tone is sharp with concern.

A wave of heat flushes my face, burning my cheeks as my eyes lock on Cain. "I, um, I'm fine..."

Eloise looks from Cain to me and back. Her eyes dip down to my baby bump. I don't miss the way her jaw drops open. I shake my head in a motion so faint it's almost imperceptible. But somehow, Eloise gets it.

"Okay. I understand." She squeezes her eyes shut and nods.

"What is it?" Garrison's voice booms.

Eloise takes my hands in hers. "It's just hot in here. Maybe we will give things a minute to calm down, there's so much commotion. What do you say Gabby? How about you and I grab some water and get some fresh air out back?"

"Yes, thank you. Let's do that."

# 53
# cain

"So how does it feel man? Twenty years and done. Full retirement at forty and a lifelong pension to go with it. You deserve it. It's time to hang out for a while." Bear Buckner claps me on the back.

"I don't know how much hanging out I'll be doing with you as my new boss. I see a whole lot of trees out there that need to be logged."

"In that case, put your gear on and get on out there." He lets out a chuckle. "But in all honesty, you should take some time for yourself first."

"Thanks, man." He's a good dude, nothing like that jackass brother of his. "I'll see you soon enough."

"Tell you what, we were out there the other day and I said to Jenkins…" Bear rambles on and I zone out.

An hour into my retirement party and this day isn't at all what I expected. I've spent the last four months dreaming of taking Gabby into my arms again. Hell, I've spent the last several years dreaming of it. Ever since she came into my world, she's all I've thought about.

But now here we are in the same space and if I didn't know better, I'd say she's avoiding me. I've caught her eye a few times only to have her look away. Meanwhile, I'm going through this room like some kind of politician, shaking hands and kissing babies.

It isn't just right now. I've felt the distance between us in her letters and on our rare phone calls. She's holding back and I'm done with it. I'm all in with Gabby and I need her to be right here with me.

I watch Gabby from across the room. She's as stunning as ever, but there's something different about her too. I can't quite put my finger on it. My eyes drift up and down her body, as the memory of her curves washes across me. As she dips into the bookshop's tiny hallway, I come back to the present. I know this is my chance to connect with her and I'm not going to let her get away this time.

"Bear, will you excuse me for a minute?"

"Yeah, of course. Don't let me keep you. We'll see you out there soon. I'll catch you up." He shakes my hand.

As soon as I'm released, I put my head down and cut a path through the crowd toward Gabby. I ignore the sound of my name being called and don't stop walking until I catch up with her in the hall.

"Gabby," I call her name, but she doesn't turn around. "Gabby." This time I grab her by the wrist and pull her back toward me.

Her face flushes deep crimson that crawls down the front of her shirt and I can't help but wonder where it stops.

"Cain." Her voice has a quiver to it. But whatever her concern, she can't hide the love in her eyes. "Hi, welcome home."

"Welcome home? That's what I get from my favorite person in the entire world." I tease her and it pulls a guarded smile from her lips.

"Stop it, there are so many people here. I can't kiss you." She hesitates, looking over her shoulder, and then lowers her voice. "But I do want to. I've missed you so much. I almost can't believe you're really back."

"Then kiss me. I don't give a shit about what any of them think... but I know you do." I turn the closest door knob. The handle opens a tiny back office with a single desk inside. I step in and pull Gabby with me. A single tug closes the door behind us. "Now I have you all to myself. Gabby, I missed you."

With the door closed, she throws her arms around my neck and I lift her off the ground. My hands roam every one of her curves and I finally feel like I'm home. I keep her pressed tight against me, squeezing her rib cage.

"Careful." She leans away from me.

"Sorry, I just can't get enough." I plant a kiss on the nape of her neck.

"I've been thinking and I need to tell you something." She chews her bottom lip.

"I've been thinking too. My favorite part of retirement is that I'm not going to miss any more nights where I can do this."

Before she can say another word, my mouth lands on her in a kiss that shoots fire through me. In an instant, Gabby and I are the only two people in the world. But the sound of the door handle turning has her jumping away from me.

"Cain the door," her voice is a whisper.

"It's locked. You're okay, I locked it. It's just us against the world." I wink at her then take her hand in mine and plant a kiss on the back of it. "What were you going to tell me?"

"I was going to say that people are probably looking for you. You are the man of the hour, don't keep them waiting." She smiles up at me, there's a flicker of something in her eyes, but I ignore it.

If I had my way, I'd stay locked in this room with her all night. But I know that isn't the reality of our situation, at least not yet.

I blow out a frustrated breath and plant a kiss on her forehead. "Okay, I'll go out first and pull all the attention. When you are ready, slip back into the party and I'll bet you no one notices. Take your time, there isn't any rush. I'm home now, for good."

She nods and purses her lips into a tight line. It takes everything in me to step out of the room and back into the party. When I do, my brother Caleb is waiting with a microphone in one hand, and a beer in the other. He waves me up to the front of the room. I grab a beer on my way because I can already tell I'm going to need it.

# 54
# gabby

"… So here's to my brother. He's a man of action and few words. Some would say, he's a man who takes the most action when others use choice words." Laughter bubbles through the crowd as Kai continues. "We're happy you're home man, we love you. Let's hear it for the big guy."

The room erupts with applause as Kai hands his microphone to Caleb. Warmth swells in my chest. For the first time in four months, I let myself feel the butterflies that flap in my stomach while I watch him accept his accolades.

Cain stands half-crooked with, a dazzling grin and chiseled jawline. I'm so proud of him for the sacrifices he's made for his country. Cain is the kind of man who changes everything he touches for the better. I'm so grateful to have him in my life.

"Let me tell you right now that you're never going to find a person more honest, more passionate, and more determined than this guy right here. I'm proud to call him my brother. We are damn lucky to have him back for good. You hear me, ladies, Cain's back and he's on the prowl."

The room erupts into laughter all over again and I feel a ridiculous pang of jealousy low in my stomach. The only thing I want him prowling is me. As soon as this party is over, I'm going to bite the bullet and tell him everything. As nervous as I am, I know it's the right thing to do. He deserves to know that our lives are about to change forever.

Caleb continues, "But I'd be kidding myself if I didn't acknowledge another incredible man who isn't here today."

The room falls silent and my heart leaps into my throat. I wrap my arms around myself in preparation for what I already know is coming.

Caleb's voice is low and somber. "Kameron should be here. If he were, he'd be standing between us no doubt. He'd be the one giving this speech and the world would be right."

The mention of Kameron's name knocks the wind out of me and I can hardly breathe. When I look up, I feel the eyes of the room turning to look at me and my throat runs dry.

Caleb continues, choking back tears. "I know he's here and I know he's proud. There ain't no doubt about that. He didn't get to chase every dream he had, but he passed so many of them along to us. He wanted our family together, happy, and healthy. He wanted Cain to retire from the Army and be home. Here we are and I know he's smiling."

Acid rises in my throat and all of a sudden, I know I'm going to be sick. I take a panicked step toward the backdoor and push it open. The crisp forest air surrounds me and I start walking. Even with the ground swirling underneath my feet, I cut a path between the trees. I don't look back until I reach the tree that took his life. He drank and drove and changed the lives of every person gathered in that room.

Angry tears stream down my face as I look at the tree. "Are you proud of me, Kameron? Are you? You're dead and your brother got me pregnant and I don't even have the decency to tell him about the baby." My words echo back to me in the emptiness.

Tears erupt from me like a fountain and once they start, I can't stop. I slump back, leaning against the tree, and sob into my palms.

"Gabby." Cain's voice in the distance has me looking up. "What the hell is wrong with you running out there like that? And how did you get so fast?"

"Cain, I'm pregnant. With your baby. You and I are going to be parents... together. I'm sorry I didn't tell you sooner, but you were gone and a part of me thought you weren't going to come back. This whole thing hasn't seemed real, but here we are. I can't ignore it anymore." As soon as the words leave my mouth, my chest loosens and I exhale.

"That's what this is about?" His jaw drops open and his eyes flicker from my face to my belly and back again.

My words hang heavy between us. I knew that setting the truth free would change everything. But I still can't say if it's for the better or the worse. I couldn't imagine anything past the absolute shock of it all. Now that I'm here, all I can do is wait. Sweat rolls down my back and I run my palms together while I give Cain time to decide our fate.

For a moment Cain rocks back onto his heels and pinches the skin between his nose. He presses his hands to his temples and walks towards me with outstretched arms. The look of shock on his face gives way to a teary-eyed smile.

"That is what this is about. It makes so much sense. How could you have thought for a single moment that I'd be anything but thrilled? This is the best thing that's ever happened to me." He blinks and two tears slip down his cheeks.

"I'm so relieved. I wasn't sure what you'd think, but I'm glad you want to do this with me."

Cain wraps me in a tight hug. "You are my whole world. I don't want anything but you all the time. The thought of you is all that got me through." He interlaces our fingers. "You are having my baby and that is the greatest gift."

I settle into Cain's arms. We stay there holding each other in silence in front of the tree that took Kameron's life. The sadness that radiates from this space starts to feel something more like peace. I imagine him right here with us, giving his blessing on this new adventure of parenthood.

Cain plants a kiss on the top of my head. "You are going to be an incredible mother. I love this baby so much already."

"I hope it's a boy and I hope he's just like you." I lean into his chest.

"We've got to get back to that party. I can't wait to tell Caleb and Kai."

At that, I sit bolt upright. "What are we going to tell everyone? They are going to think it's super weird... Maybe we can make a plan about when we'll tell them. You know, down the line when baby is old enough to tell them himself."

Cain firmly takes my hand and starts walking back up the path in the direction of the bookshop. "I know that your parents have done a real number on you over the years. But I'm going to tell you something about the group of people in that bookshop. They love you. Period. There aren't any conditions tied to it. I know that might be hard for you to believe, but it's the truth. I'm going to prove it to you. Right now. That's it, let's go."

I couldn't pull my hand away if I tried. Cain marches us back toward the doors of the bookshop and my throat runs dry. He pulls the door open without hesitation and steps inside, pulling me in behind him.

# 55
# cain

I shove the door open and head for the microphone at the front of the room. The wide-eyed panic on Gabby's face doesn't go unnoticed, but it doesn't slow me down. If this is what's coming between us, then the issue has to be addressed. We don't have a second to waste. Our relationship is bigger than the two of us now, we're going to be parents.

"Y'all listen up." My words explode out of me louder than I mean them to and the bookshop falls pin drop silent. I wait until all eyes are on us and pull Gabby tightly to my side. Her palm is warm and I can feel her breath come in quick gasps. I lower my voice and turn away from the microphone. "You're going to be just fine. I need you to trust me."

"Okay," is all she says in response.

I clear my throat. "I'm going to make this short and sweet. Me and Gabby are in love... With each other. We have been for a long while now."

The last murmurs of conversation come to a screeching halt. Every single person in the room is staring at me, most of them with open mouths. I know this is Gabby's nightmare, but it's the start of my wildest dream. Gabby is the most incredible woman I've ever known. She's already changed my world by being in it and that's something to be proud of.

I continue, "I know that some of you probably don't understand. Let me explain this to you. Back when she was Kameron's fiance, I thought Gabby was one hell of a cool person. As it turns out, I was right. But back then, we were friends and nothing more. After we lost Kameron, God bless my brother, everything changed. Gabby and I grew closer. We helped each other through the loss of our lives. In that time, I found my other half and I'm so grateful for that."

I run my thumb over the back of Gabby's hand. When she looks up at me, the fear in her eyes is still there, only now there's something else too. *Is it hope? Is it trust in me?* The thoughts make my heart swell in my chest.

"Go on," there's a quiver to her voice.

"What I also found is the strongest woman you've ever met. She's sweet and thoughtful. I don't know if you know this, but she can make damn near anything out of yarn. Gabby is all that's kept me going on that long final deployment." I plant a kiss on the top of her head. "I need you all to know that whatever you think of our situation, I love Gabby with all my heart. If any of you don't like that, you can see the door located right behind me."

It catches me off-guard when for a long while, the room stays silent. I'm met with nothing but wide eyes and slack jaws. Gabby's shoulders pull back and she doesn't try to take her hand away. We are in this now, the two of us against—

*Clap. Clap. Clap.*

Finally, Eloise breaks the ice and more clapping follows. She raises her glass. "Cheers to the happy couple."

"Cheers," Garrison follows suit. But the tight lines on his face tell me that a conversation between the two of us is in order.

He's protective of his sister and I'm okay with that. Garrison deserves to know that I'll take care of his sister after all she's been through. Still seeing his reaction reminds me that there is still one more detail to share and Garrison might not like what's coming.

The tension breaks in the room as congratulations come in waves of soft murmurs. But I'm not done yet.

Without giving it another thought, I let the other shoe drop. "Also... We're having a baby and I couldn't be happier. I just thought y'all might want to know."

This time there isn't any silence. The room erupts with congratulations in an instant. Gabby lets out a deep sigh and buries her face in my chest as I wrap my arms around her.

I hold the microphone up to my mouth one last time and take a deep breath. I look Gabby in the eyes. "I love you unconditionally and with my whole heart. I commit my life to loving you and this baby. You won't want for anything. Will you marry me?"

# 56
# epilogue: gabby

"You can set them up here any way you'd like, it won't matter too much, I know they're going to fly off the shelf." Ariella claps her hands. "I mean who doesn't need a tiny crocheted axe? Are you kidding me right now? These are so stinking cute."

"I hope you're right." With twin boys at home, I'm not going to return to my actual job anytime soon. I wouldn't want it any other way. There are too many precious moments to miss a single one. "Thanks again for letting me do this."

"Of course! I can't wait to take a picture for the website as soon as you have them arranged."

"I'm on it asap." I pull a pair of crocheted beards out of the box. But even as the words leave my mouth, I know they aren't exactly true. I'm not going to move quickly. This is one of my first trips without the babies and I needed the peace more than I realized.

The sound of the Tortured Poets Department playing softly in the background is the only thing breaking the silence here and it feels like a warm hug. As I organize my handmade creations onto the shelves, my heart swells with gratitude for the life I've been given in Lumberjack Lagoon. It doesn't look the way I'd imagined, but somehow it's better than anything I could have dreamed up.

Motherhood suits me. I instantly felt a connection to these two little babies who represent the best parts of me and their father. Every breath, every minute feels like a gift. The babies have brought Cain and me closer than ever. My only wish is for time to slow down.

Being a father has made Cain more of who he already was. He's more protective, more thoughtful, more determined to show up for me in every way. Right now our nights are sleepless but our days are overflowing with love.

It's incredible how my one heart has expanded to love my two little guys in completely different ways. Little Gari Bear is a spitting image of me with his deep and pooling eyes and his full head of wild curls. He laughs easily and only wants to be in my arms as much as possible. On the other hand, Little Kammer is stoic and sure of himself. His exploration of the world around him never ceases, he is just like his father.

When Cain suggested we name our sons after their uncles, I knew it was the right decision. It's a gift for both Cain and me to have such a special connection to our pasts. No matter how anyone else feels about it, Kam is a part of Cain's and my perfectly imperfect love story. Now the bond that we have with Kam will continue not only in our hearts but into our future through these little guys.

These babies will grow up surrounded by a legacy of strong men and I know Kameron is up there smiling down on us as we speak.

*Ding.*

I turn at the sound of the bell chiming against the bookshop's front door. Cain steps inside in his lumberjack gear. The sight of him sweaty in his skin-tight white shirt never gets old.

"Wait, where are the babies?"

Cain's eyes lock on mine and he makes his way towards me. "Your brother and Eloise are taking them for the night."

"What? What are you doing?"

"I'm doing you." His words are a growl as he wraps his arms around me and I melt into his embrace.

# bonus story: hank hemlock applies for the golden bachelor

# part one, hank

"Okay!" Ariella Greenwood steps back from the mirror and holds her scissors up in triumph. "You look amazing. Now put on the clothes I bought you and meet me down at the bookshop just before sunset. They call it golden hour for a reason. It's going to be perfect."

"Yeah well, I call it dinner time. I look ridiculous with this damn haircut."

"Oh come on now Hank, how are you going to win the heart of a gorgeous lady with that surly attitude?" She brushes clippings of hair from my shoulders. "You lumberjacks are all the same."

"Whoa, first off, I am not a lumberjack. You have to admit this whole thing is wild. Back in my day, you met a woman the way you were. There was no need for shaving and combing, and special shirts that itch when you wear them." My words come out in a low grumble, but Ariella has gotten good at ignoring me since we've become *friends*.

Instead of answering my protests, she holds up her hands excitedly one last time. Then she collects her things and bounds toward my front door, her pink bag slug across her shoulder. "See you tonight!"

"Yeah, okay."

When my door closes, I can't help but smile. As much as I resisted her intrusion into my life, it's been nice to have people in and out of my house. Ariella, her sister Nadia, and their husbands have become more like family to me. It's still hard for me to believe. I'm not used to being a part of a group like this. It's been a long time since I've gotten an invitation anywhere... I know I don't have anyone to blame but myself for that.

I know what they say about me in town, *slum lord, creepy old man, bad guy.* Hell when I first met Ariella, she thought I might off her somewhere in the forest. When she asked about me in town, not a single person could give her a reason to believe she might be wrong. The people of Lumberjack Lagoon have a way of blowing things out of proportion. But they aren't all wrong. I've done things I'm not proud of over the years. But anyone in my position would have done the same thing, I'm sure of it.

Contrary to popular belief, I did love once. Back before any of these lumberjacks were old enough to swing an axe I was just a normal guy that got dealt a shit hand by life. I didn't set out to become the villain.

There was a time when innocence still existed in me. It was before the wrinkles, leathery skin, and isolation. It was back before I understood what people are capable of. I never wanted to end up like this, but life's cruel twists molded me into this unrecognizable shell of a human being.

Once upon a time, I was a young, quiet, and awkward man. Some would even say I was handsome, but there aren't many pictures to go on. I was on my way home from my job as a ranch hand when I cut a path through the woods. I thought I'd find some extra daylight by getting home a few minutes early. Instead, I found a woman who changed everything.

# part two, hank

I'll never forget the first time I laid eyes on Clemmie. She was nothing more than a dark silhouette standing against the sparkling lagoon. But I was inexplicably drawn to her. She had a wicker basket overflowing with wildflowers on her arm and her long hair blew in the breeze. She looked like she was straight from a storybook, and there weren't many fairy tales in my life at that point.

When I got closer, she introduced herself as Clementine Hughes. She said she was new to town and I felt like the luckiest man on the planet to be the among the first people to meet her. Clemmie's skin was smooth and pale. Her hair glimmered in shades of rich auburn that matched the falling leaves on the trees and I was enamored. From the moment our eyes met, I was desperate for more of her. I'd fallen completely under her spell.

I set out to do the impossible. I decided to make Clemmie mine. We took to meeting deep in the woods only sit together and talk for hours. Clemmie was a few years older than me. She didn't have many friends. She told me that girls tended to be jealous of her, and I could see it. She had everything, beauty, brains... the whole package. She told me that men only wanted to sleep with her. A pang of guilt washed over me as I swallowed back my own intentions.

Her parents were tough on her, so I did what I could to help her stay out of her house for long stretches of time. It was no surprise that her folks didn't even want to meet me, but that didn't bother me. I didn't have a family of my own so their rejection felt like par for the course.

I ran away from a group home at fourteen and never looked back. I didn't know my father and my mother was an alcoholic teenager who left me at a fire station from what I'd heard. Telling Clemmie about my past felt like freedom. It was exhilarating. The sparks shooting back and forth between us was pure magic.

Through the abuse and chaos of a family-less life, I'd always been determined that my ending would be different than my beginning. I knew I'd work hard. I'd stay on the straight and narrow. One day I would make my own stability. Clemmie was the final piece of the puzzle and I got to work. Somehow, little by little, I did it. I got Clemmie to fall in love with me.

I was accustomed to a life of lonliness. Having Clemmie by my side felt like reparations for all the injustices I'd suffered. By then, I was almost eighteen years old and I thought I'd found myhappy ending. For two whole years, we hid away in a tiny A-framed cabin at the bottom of a hill tucked into the forest. The place wasn't ours, but Clemmie broke the window and we lived like we hadn't a care in the world, destined for happily ever after.

Of course, nothing is perfect. Clemmie had needs. She grew up poor and that bothered her. She had a tendency to gravitate towards the finer things in life and I couldn't hold that against her. It's a feeling I understood. I'd work as hard as I needed to to give her the life she deserved.

But Clemmie wasn't a patient woman. Her wants came with a hefty price tag I wasn't prepared to pay. First, it was a demand for more of the basics; cash for food, a new bike, a journal to scribble down her poetry. These weren't a problem. I took extra shifts at the farm and got a second job working part time at the local diner washing dishes. It felt good to be the man making her dreams come life... But it wasn't enough.

Clemmie moved on to needing expensive clothing, then jewelry. She wanted a car and to start getting her hair done. Every time I scrapped together the means to meet her needs, the list grew. I knew that if I wanted to keep Clemmie in my life, I had to find a way to make more money. She wasn't going to stick around while I climbed the ladder of hierarchy at the farm.

I wasn't naive. I knew there were faster ways of getting Clemmie everything she ever wanted. But I wanted to stay on the right side of the law. Growing up an orphan had given me a front-row seat to the things desperate people can do to get ahead. It's a cycle I was desperate not to repeat.

The first crime I committed was small. I swiped the cash from the register after a shift at the diner. It was almost too easy. No one saw me. Pinning the blame on old Joan was simple because people already hated her. They were looking for evidence to justify their judgments of her. I handed it to them on a platter. Joan was a thief.

Only, she wasn't. She was a smoker and a yeller, with one hell of an aggressive mole on her chin. But truth be told Joan wasn't a bad person. Being accused of stealing from a place she'd worked for over twenty years sent her into an early retirement she couldn't afford. I felt bad on the day it all played out. But if I had it to do over, I'd have made the same decisions. Given the choice between old lady Joan and Clemmie, there wasn't any question about where my loyalties were.

Once I crossed that bridge there wasn't any going back. Committing small crimes got progressively easier and the payoffs got bigger. I was on a path to becoming exactly who the group home managers always thought I'd be; *a bad guy, a loser, someone who no one cared about.*

Worse, lit seemed like fate. Going with the grain instead of against it made me feel like, I finally wasn't swimming up stream. Living a life of petty crime on the fringes of society fit me like a glove. It was my natural state of being, and from there, things only escalated.

Petty theft escalated into a sophisticated loan sharking scheme, followed by more white-collar crimes. After a particularly successful money laundering operation, I bought Clemmie the cabin of her dreams complete with fifty-three acres of forest all around it.

The place was a true luxury escape overlooking the lagoon. It had gardens, tennis courts, and a fountain that made your jaw drop. But I didn't stop there. My next purchase was the A-frame cabin Clemmie and I spent our early years squatting in. I left the cabin as was, but I built out a massive greenhouse right behind it.

My rise to success by any means was lightning fast. Somehow, it was still not fast enough for Clemmie. By then, the cracks in our relationship had started to show. Her behavior had become erratic. She'd drive by my workplace and threaten any woman within a hundred yards of me, even though I'd never had eyes for anyone but her. She'd tell me that I was her hero in one breath and in the next, she'd ask why I didn't love her enough to give her what she wanted.

Toying with my emotions became a game for Clemmie. She'd come up with these outlandish needs and she'd tell me it was my job to find a way to make them happen. Then she'd assign an arbitrary deadline to to topic and leave me love notes signed, *tik-tok.*

Clemmie loved the power she held over me. It excited her to watch me scramble. I'd fall for her traps every time because I thought that's what love was. After all, I didn't have anything to compare it to.

When Clemmie's demands became so outlandish that I put my foot down and resisted, Clemmie had a solution for that too. She'd drop to her knees and beg me to get her what she wanted with my dick in her mouth. She was all long hair and fluttering eyelashes as she sucked me off gagging before telling me to cum down her throat. For a man who spent his life alone, that kind of attention was intoxicating. It's all she needed to pull me right back under her spell.

Our relationship was Clemmie against the world and Clemmie who was my world. So you can imagine my surprise when I found out that my Clemmie, who I sacrificed everything for, was in love with a fucking lumberjack of all people.

# part three, hank

She didn't lead with the truth. I have no idea how long the overlap between me and lumberjack was. Was he around in the shadows for a week? A year? Even if she had been honest with me, I might not have accepted it. I was blinded by my adoration for her. I was stupid. I couldn't see the lies that were sitting right in front of my face and that's exactly the way she wanted it.

Clemmie simply told me that she was bored of me and of the life we'd scraped together. She told me to sell everything and take her on a trip around the world. When I agreed she said that maybe we'd be better off staying put. The back and forth was impossible. I knew we had problems, but Clemmie was the person who had been in my life the longest and I never considered she wanted someone else.

In the end, she grew bored of the games. Clemmie uttered a casual comment over a bowl of cereal that reverberates in my mind to this day. "I've met someone and he's a lumberjack, and he's such a *good* man."

The irony slapped me across the face. Clemmie wanted a *good guy* when she single-handedly turned me into a fucking nightmare of a person.

My heart shattered into a million pieces. I wanted to hate her, to be angry and move on. But instead, I only felt desperate to get her back. I begged and pleaded with her to stay and to give me another chance. I promised her I'd do anything to make her happy. But all she could do was shrug and shake her head.

I was used to watching Clemmie destroy people, but I never thought she'd turn on me. Yet, here I was. My world crumbled around me. This lumberjack wasn't rich or privileged. He was just your run-of-the-mill blue collar dude with a big axe.

When Clemmie was moving out of our mansion and into his tiny two bedroom cabin, Mr. Oakes came to defend her honor. He took his life in his hands to tell me that he wasn't going to stand for the way I'd treated Clemmie. I was too shocked to be mad. I'd treated her like the only person who had ever loved me, like an absolute queen. As he kept talking, so many of the stories she told me about her parents came back. Only this time, I was the bad guy in them.

He hurled false accusations at me one after the next and I stood there, taking it, dumfounded.Looking back I should have felt bad for the guy. Whatever she sold him, he bought hook line, and sinker. Instead all I could think about is the way Clemmie probably used that same pretty little mouth that she loved to wrap around my dick to win his affection and the thought made me sick.

My love was nothing more than a snake, slithering away into the darkness. She was one more person who didn't think I was worth staying for. It destroyed me. The loss of Clemmie filled me with betrayal, pain, and a complete disdain for lumberjacks. And yet, even as I bled out on the floor, a twisted part of me still longed to have her back, to do anything for her, no matter how much it destroyed me.

Clemmie taught me that it isn't only the nice guys who finish last. It's a lesson I vowed to learn only once. I set out to live in stony isolation and accumulate wealth through any means necessary. That's exactly what I did. I've burned a hell of a lot of people along the way.

As for the lumberjack, Mr. Oakes, I wasn't prepared to let him off the hook without teaching him a lesson. He needed to know who he was stealing from. So I started digging into his life.

The decision about how to hurt him was an easy one. If this man was going to swoop into my world and take my Clemmie, it would leave my heart frozen in time. In return, the only thing I could do was make sure the town he loved suffered the same fate.

I liquidated Clemmie's dream house and used the money to scoop up every ounce of property in Lumberjack Lagoon. I laughed to myself when I heard locals talk about the mystery buyer and what they hoped would happen to the property. *I hope it's a drive-in, I hope it's a new shopping center, maybe it will be a hotel.* None of their hopes would come true, I'd make sure of that.

It wasn't just the lumberjack. As time when on, I decided it was nice to have the power for once. I wanted to pay back the town that had done so little for me over the years. So I kept purchasing. I planned to do absolutely nothing with the land. I was going to hold it hostage.

I bought business' and raised the rent until they couldn't keep the doors open. Before I knew it, downtown Lumberjack Lagoon was a ghost town. I'd frozen the industry of the entire town outside of the logging company. If my heart was going to be stuck in a sand timer, then so were they.

I never talked to Clemmie again. She tried to come back into my world a few times, but I knew better than to re-open that door. That doesn't mean I didn't watch her, I did. I could never quite turn away from her completely.

I got no satisfaction from watching the way she grew tired of the good guys. She was over Mr. Oakes in six months flat, but the lumberjack thing stuck. I watched her pattern over and over again though the years. They'd start strong and within a few weeks, you'd catch word of a heartbroken man with a whole lot of money missing. A few of the dudes even came knocking on my door after she'd taken them for all they had. But I wasn't in the mood to commiserate.

There guys were nothing like me. They may have given Clemmie some of what they had, but I can't imagine they let her change who they were. She reserved that for me. I kept all my hate bottled up and all to myself for all these years.

But all that changed when Clemmie passed away. She died unmarried and alone. Without anyone to throw a wake, her name was nothing more than a mark in the local paper. I went out to our A-frame cabin and spent the night crying like a baby.

Clemmie was a troubled woman who only knew how to take. Knowing that she was finally at peace made me question wether or not it was too late for me to learn how to give.

# part four, hank

Clemmie has always had a way of spurring me into action and her death didn't change that. As soon as I left our tiny A-frame, I got to work with letting go and moving on.

It isn't happening overnight. There are a lot of bridges burned and Lord knows there aren't any secrets in this town. Every skeleton I have has a way of making it out of the closet and onto the timber yard in Lumberjack Lagoon. But I own that, and it hasn't stopped me from trying to fix things.

For starters, I sold half the hillside and a shack of a cabin that was on it to a man who turned the place into a lodge for billionaires. I don't love the idea even now, but I can't deny that it's created a lot of tourism in our town. It was a good step in bringing this place back to life.

From there, I donated the storefronts downtown to a new initiative that aims to rebuild local small businesses. From what I can tell, it seems to be working. The place is lined with cars like I haven't seen in years. Another fact I'm not crazy about.

With each restoration project, the towns icy perception of me thaws just a little. I like the feeling of being included more than I'm willing to admit.

I didn't think I'd be able to part ways with the old A-frame cabin. It was too special, sacred even. I wasn't ready to sell it to just anyone. But I know I'm not going to be around forever. If I didn't get it into the right hands, it would surely be destroyed when I pass.

The day Ariella Greenwood contacted me about the listing, it only took one conversation to know she was the right person. There was something about the desperation in her tone that told me she was the right one. I've learned to trust my intuition over the years and this time, I was right.

Ariella offered me a fraction of what the land was worth and I took it without hesitation. I made it seem like she was doing me a favor in helping me unload the place. She's done one hell of a job letting that little cabin live it's destiny. She even turned the greenhouse out back into a bookshop. She calls it, *The Lumberjack Hideaway.*

Even though I cringed at the irony of my cabin with Clemmie being named after a damn lumberjack, I can admit it feels right.

Of course the transition wasn't completely smooth. It was odd for me to think of someone else living in the only place I've ever felt loved. When Ariella first moved in, I couldn't stop myself from lingering on the property. It didn't do anything to help my reputation for being creepy.

Eventually she got sick of my lingering around outside of her house. She thought it was about her. Ariella actually thought that I gave two shits what she does with her days. When she bypassed her lumberjack of a husband to confront me herself, I could hardly contain my laughter. Ariella's tiny balled fists pelted my chest, demanding to know what I wanted from her.

Even more surprising than seeing her fly out of the house after me, is the fact that I told her. There was something about the honestly in Ariella's line of questioning that only left room for the truth. When I told her everything, Ariella's face washed with sympathy and understanding. Instead of demanding that I leave, she told me that I'm welcome any time.

Somehow between scolding me and learning the history of the cabin, Ariella and I formed a friendship. She's even helped others come around to the idea that I'm a changed man set of righting my wrongs. It's give me a place to belong like I've never experienced. That's exactly how I ended up dressed like a complete fool with a tie on over my flannel when I meet Ariella at the bookshop behind the A-frame cottage.

The idea of going on a date after all this time has nerves rattling in my stomach. I suspect it's a blind date and that's okay with me. Even if she doesn't like me, I've got to start somewhere. For the first time in my life, I have a place to belong. I feel ready to bring someone new into my life. It took me long enough to get here. All I want to do is spend the rest of my life with a true love.

I take a deep breath before I push open the door of the bookshop. My eyes roam the shelves looking for a woman of a certain age… Only Ariella is all alone.

"Don't you look handsome," she beams at me.

I cut my eyes at her. "Well, where is she?" Nerves make my words come out in a bark.

"Hank… Where is who?" Ariella bounds around the counter toward me.

"My date. I didn't get dressed up for you… No offense."

"None taken." She smiles and shakes her head. "That isn't how it works these days. We are going to get you set up using this." Ariella points at her computer.

I let out a frustrated breath. "No way. I'm not going all in just to have some weirdo show up. Don't you know that people on the intra-net can say whatever the hell they want?" I throw my hands up in protest. "They call it catfishing."

She lets out a giggle. "Stop it. You aren't making an online dating profile. You're applying to be the next Golden Bachelor. It's a show where—"

"Ha! I know what the hell it is. I'm old, not dead. Everyone watched Gary find love," I grumble.

She bites back another laugh, though I have no idea what's so funny. "You would make for incredible TV is all I'm saying. I needed you to dress up so we can capture some photos. Golden hour in the forest is the perfect time and place for a photoshoot. Between Lumberjack Lodge being all the craze with the rich and famous and the fact that you've been single for over a decade, you're going to be the ideal candidate. Let's get the pictures done and then we'll finish your application."

"What do you mean finish the application?"

"Oh, I've answered all the basic questions for you, but you're going to have to finish a few of these yourself..."

# hank's application questions

**Why would you want to find love on TV?**

I don't particularly care for "on tv" part personally. But I've been told that this is how people find each other these days and I'm willing to do whatever it takes. I deserve love dammit, I've been alone for far too long.

**How many relationships have you had?**

One, but it was doozy. Set me back for a long time.

**Why did it end?**

It ended because of a damn lumberjack. This town I live in is riddled with them. I've found a few recently that aren't all that bad. But most of them are something to look out for. They're walking around with plaid and swinging big axes. Makes you wonder what they're compensating for if you ask me.

**What are your relationship deal breakers?**

I don't want anyone who likes lumberjacks, climbing, axes, or trees. She's got to be a person who appreciates the simple things in life like taking walks in the forest. It doesn't hurt if she's something to look at... you know what I mean. Curvy. Full figured is what I used to call it.

**Have you ever auditioned for a reality show before? Explain.**

You must be kidding me. No, I have not because I'm not an asshat. Can't hardly believe I'm doing it now. I'm not exactly sure what this means, but I've been told I will make good tv.

**Are you genuinely looking for love? Explain why.**

Of course, I am. Do you think I would be going through all this bullshit if I wasn't? I've waited a long time for this and I'm ready. I've got a nice home and a makeshift family for the first time in my life. Anybody would be lucky to be a part of it. I know how to treat my woman. Now I want to meet someone who will love me for who I am. I'm not polished and fancy, but there's no question that when I meet the one who is meant for me, I will spend the rest of my life making sure she knows that she's the most important person. I hope I get the chance.

---

**Subscribe to my newsletter** and get a free lumberjack book sent straight to your inbox

**Shop directly with Elsie** for more exclusive products and discounted bundles!

**Ready for more?** Get ready to meet the mountain men of Brew by Brewer

# about the author

I'm Elsie & I'm so happy you're here, you're going to fall in love tonight💕

I write short & steamy small-town romance stories about mountain men, lumberjacks, and ranchers. If you are looking to escape reality and fall into the arms of a man who will never let you down, you've come to the right place.

All of my books come with the promise of relatable characters, funny dialogue, no cheating, no cliffhangers & a happily ever after 💋

***You deserve to treat yourself to falling in love with your new book boyfriend!***

Hugs,

Elsie James

💋 ***Subscribe to my Newsletter and get a FREE EBook sent straight to your inbox!***

💋 Access exclusive deals when you shop directly with Elsie!

💋 Grab more delicious Bonus Content when you join the Treat Team as a FREE member on Patreon!

💋 Learn more: https://elsiejamesauthor.com/

www.ingramcontent.com/pod-product-compliance
Lightning Source LLC
Jackson TN
JSHW021853130425
82456JS00001B/4
* 9 7 9 8 2 3 0 8 9 7 1 2 5 *